Imagine If

Imagine if everything that happened in your life happened for a reason. **Imagine if** life on earth was just a dress rehearsal for the spiritual world. **Imagine if** every life event that had occurred, will repeat itself with repercussions on the next level of life's journey. **Imagine if** you found out that your life has meaning in the afterlife. **Imagine if** you found out every life has a meaning and every action has a consequence.

Imagine if is about Curtis Schmidt's life struggle with depression and how he questioned everything about his life. He didn't understand why everything seemed to turn out wrong. What happened the day he fell through the ice? What happened on the job interview after college? Why couldn't he save his unborn child? Why did his marriage fail? Why did he lose his job? Why did God fail him? These questions are answered when he meets in his afterlife, his long lost child, his parents, his grandfather, Jesus Christ and God on a journey of answers to the questions of all the misery suffered when he was alive, and the reasons why. He finds himself facing his own life decisions in Purgatory and ends up facing his own Hell. Only in Hell can Curtis Schmidt come to grips that his life and every life matters.

DEDICATED TO:

I would like to dedicate this book to Taylor, Mike, and my Mom and Dad. All of you have left this earth way too young.

Taylor, you lost your battle with Leukemia 10 years ago. You showed us how to fight for everyday of our lives. You are an inspiration to all. Because of you, there isn't a day that goes by that I forget to tell my own children I love them, because I'm afraid to lose even one day. Your short time on earth taught us all what is really important in life.

Mike, your incredible smile and attitude taught us how to live life. I wish I had your outlook on life. You fought cancer and beat it, always being upbeat and positive. Unfortunately, your large heart gave out way too soon.

Mom and Dad, I hope you're able to see my beautiful children from Heaven. In many ways, they are just like the two of you. The goodness in you now shines in them. I miss you and love you both.

IMAGINE

Imagine all the people living life in peace. You may say I'm a dreamer, but I'm not the only one. I hope someday you'll join us, and the world will be as one.

~John Lennon

Prologue

Raising his arm high in the air, Curt's unconstrained perspiration burst off his body onto the gymnasium floor, leaving a trail from half court to the rim. Unable to speak, because of shortness of breath from running up and down the floor, all he could do is raise his arm hoping his teammate and friend Mike would spot him open. Mike smiled as he threw the basketball down the court, forcing his friend to exert additional energy to reach the ball. With a couple of steps on his opponent, Curt reached the ball dribbled twice and carefully completed his layup for what should have been an easy basket. The ball hit the backboard, hit the front of the rim and rolled off, allowing his opponent to grab the rebound, toss the ball down court to an open teammate who was able to complete his layup and win the pickup game for his team. Curt stood under the basket winded as Mike jogged over to him, patting him on the back, and stated "Nice shot! So what was that, like 0 for 40 this game?"

Curt just lifted his head, still gasping for air, before dropping it and shaking it side to side. "God, I suck at this game."

Mike was laughing. "You're really, really not good. Maybe you should stick to lying on the couch." Mike and Curt both looked at the other team signaling that they were done for the night. "Seriously, though, you need to get in better shape. You're gonna have a heart attack out here."

"I'll start training for the marathon tomorrow. Right now, I need a shower and a beer."

Mike slapped Curt in the gut, "I'm not sure you need a beer, it looks like you have a half keg their already." Mike looked at his hand looking for a place to wipe Curt's sweat from his palm, before reluctantly wiping the sweat on his shorts.

"1/2 Keg now, 6 pack not too long ago."

"Curt, we've been friends over 30 years, and you never had a six pack, unless it was from your refrigerator."

"Wow, with comments like that, I can't imagine being friends for 30 minutes with you, let alone 30 years." Curt stopped near the water fountain outside the boy's locker room and grabbed a drink, wiping the excess water off with his forearm. "30 years is a long time. Remember the first time we met? I just moved in and some jerk challenged me to a fight. We rolled from one side of the lawn to the other, neither one throwing a punch. Eventually, the rolling stopped and you cried like a baby to get me off of you."

"...actually Curt, you ran home crying. I guess I hurt your feelings."

"Nope, don't remember that."

"Then you must remember dating the most beautiful girls at school, winning the lottery, winning a Grammy and a Nobel peace prize. Oh, that's right those things didn't happen either." Mike's grin grew with every word out of his mouth.

Curt looked Mike straight in the eyes, "That was hurtful. Very, hurtful."

"Get dressed you big baby, and I'll buy my unemployed friend a beer."

"Again, hurtful!"

Having lost his job a few days earlier, still stung with Curt. Mike had a way of taking any situation and making every situation seem like it would be okay. Curt on the other hand, believed that the world was out to get him. He would tell everyone, "Just because I'm paranoid, doesn't mean people aren't out to get me." Mike was clearly a half glass full type of guy and Curt was hoping to be at least half empty. The two were a perfect balance of Yin Yang energy.

The two got dressed and headed to Morrissey's for a couple of beers. They sat at the bar watching the Yankees game on the big screen, with Curt becoming more frustrated as his beloved Red Sox found another way to lose to Mike's Yankees. "That's twenty bucks you owe me. Pay up sucka."

Curt pulled the twenty out of his wallet, leaving only 11 bucks left and handed the money to Mike. "Man, I wonder what I did wrong in my previous life to deserve every possibility of misery in this life."

"Curt, you gotta relax. You're just too hard on yourself. What you need to do…" as Mike's sentenced was interrupted by a fight between two guys he had never met before.

The two men who knew of each other began fighting over a woman, who wasn't present. It seems the husband of the woman came looking for this guy and jumped him from behind, hitting him in the back of the head, before tossing him to the ground. The blonde guy in his early thirties, swung his body, kicking his feet in an attempt to get up, but the larger gentleman grabbed him and threw him across a table, spilling and breaking the pitcher of beer and glasses as the blonde gentleman was too hurt and cut up to move. "Now punk, you're gonna get what you deserve. Nobody screws with my wife. YOUR'RE DEAD." The enraged man pulled out a switchblade and headed directly at the man on the ground.

Curt froze not knowing what to do. Mike jumped off his barstool and yelled "Enough," as he positioned himself between the two men. The man swung the blade at Mike's chest forcing Mike to move away. Mike then pushed the momentum of the man's arm away from his core balance and moved his leg between the man's throwing the man to the ground. The burly dark haired man screamed in anger attempting to get up when Mike slammed down his knee on the man's chest, then punching the man twice in the face before disengaging the blade from his hand. In the end Mike sat on the man's neck and chest, holding the man, now with the help of other bar patrons until the police came. In the end, Mike and Curt left the bar, having to stay later than expected.

"Man, I don't get you. You could've been killed by that guy. Here you have everything to lose, I have nothing and you put it all out there."

"Don't be so hard on yourself. I happened to see what was going on. You had your back initially to them. You would've done the same."

"I don't think so. Once he pulled that knife, images of my kids ran through my head."

Mike paused for a moment. "Funny thing, I had images of the blonde dude's kids going through my head and not my own kids." Mike thought for another moment as they walked to their car, "If I had thought first of my kids, I'm not sure if I would have reacted."

Both were silent as they got to Mike's Ford Mustang. Mike pressed the keyless remote opening all the locks and Curt jumped right in. Curt looked over at the half opened driver's door, wondering why Mike didn't get in. "Now where is he?" Curt got out of the car and headed back around the car when he seen Mike lying on the ground motionless. "MIKE, OH my God! MIKE?" Curt rolled him over and felt no pulse. For a moment, he didn't know if he should start CPR, but noticed the ambulance hadn't left with the blonde man being treated for his wounds. Curt screamed to the paramedics to run over. Curt began CPR on his friend who saved a man's life earlier, who now needed to be saved himself.

Curt wasn't a hero, as Mike was buried three days later.

Chapter 1 Comfort of My Bed

Curt watched, in his SpongeBob underwear, his kids get on their morning school bus. He pointed to his eye and to his heart before pointing to his daughter, then repeating the same motion to his son, adding two fingers at the end. Both his children smiled as they mimicked I love you and I love you too symbols back to their dad. The only difference is they both wiggled their fingers and spread their arms out wide, stating I love you a bazillion times.

As the bus pulled away from the front of the house Curt closed the door and thought of what he could accomplish that day. "Should I work on my resume? Should I cut the lawn?" Instead he decided to walk back to the bedroom and flop down face first on his bed. He thought about Mike for awhile, before his mind wandered on him needing a job.

Having been fired really affected Curt. He seemed to have it all just a few short years earlier. Curt had a beautiful house, a beautiful family and friends, a good paying job that allowed him to save for the future and provide whatever needs his kids had.   In an instant, it was all gone.

His wife had left when she met another man at the health club. After the kids were born, she felt fat and hated her body. She decided to join a health club to help her get back in the shape she was before she had kids. Curt was supportive, taking care of the young children, while his wife worked out. At first, she would go after dinner, somehow leaving a pile of dishes for Curt to clean. She would be gone a couple of hours, before coming home a little more refreshed.

Curt didn't mind the arrangement of 3 or 4 days a week, because it gave him quality time with his children. Curt was there when his little girl rolled over for the first time. Curt was there for his son's first steps. They would play games and read books while mommy was away. They grew an incredible bond.

The workouts which began around six slowly began creeping up to her coming home at 9. Curt thought at first the workouts must be getting more intense, until she began coming home after 10. Christy would tell Curt that she went out for a few drinks with the girls afterward. Soon Friday nights, she didn't come home until 1 or 2 am and Curt knew in his gut that more was going on than just a night out with the girls, from the health club, for a few drinks. He trusted his wife, yet he couldn't shake this feeling.

"Did you check your wife's underwear drawer?" Bill suggested as he had talked to his best friend at work one day about Christy coming home later and later. "Ask any of the driver's here who have gotten divorced recently. Everyone checked their wives underwear drawer only to see brand new underwear that they never seemed before."

"So?" a look of confusion on Curt's face. "I have new underwear in my drawer. So what?"

"When was the last time you seen your wife come to bed in brand new sexy underwear. You know a nice red thong? You mentioned she's been going out a lot. Do you think if she's not having an affair or at least thinking about having an affair, she would need to buy new underwear. How about her bras, I'll bet that they are all brand new too."

"I don't think I ever seen her buy a bra. Her mother always seems to get them for her for Christmas. I think she has like one nice laced red bra from our honeymoon. The rest are granny purchased bras."

"I'm tellin' you straight up. If she has her typical white silky, stained, with holes underwear in the drawer, your marriage is safe. If it looks as if she just bought out Victoria Secrets and you haven't seen any of it on her, you've got a problem."

Curt went home that night, ate dinner with his wife and kids, did the dishes as his wife went to work out and proceeded to play with the kids. At 8:30 he put the kids to bed and headed into his bedroom. He walked around the bed to his wife's dresser and opened the top drawer on the right. There was his answer, brand new colorful thongs that he never seen his wife in. His jaw dropped and the feelings of a 14 year old boy came across him as if his first ever love broke his heart again. "She's having an affair", Curt stated out loud as to give it more credibility by hearing his own voice. "No, no, I've been good, it's just a coincidence. " Trying to make himself believe that there had to be another explanation. Curt proceeded to open the center drawer on the dresser and proceeded to look at his wife's bras. "Oh my God," as he picked up all the brand new low cut lacey bra's in black shear, red, navy blue, and a multi faceted collection of bras he clearly would have noticed on his wife. "She's not only having an affair, she's freakin hot for this guy."

The following day he was met at work by his friend Bill and 3 other co-workers who were recently divorced or separated. "By the look on your face you found new underwear. Sorry guy." As Bill placed his hand on Curt's shoulder. "We've all been there."

"There was so much lace in the bras, so little parts to the underwear. " Curt described the horrific seen as if it were a plane crash he had witnessed.

"Has she been side kissing you?" asked Dylan an accountant who was recently divorced.

"What?" Curt looking up to find out that there was more nerve wrecking news he wasn't prepared for.

"You know the side kiss. You walk in from work and your kids greet you at the door, you hug and kiss them, you walk over to your wife and instead of kissing lips on lips, she turns her cheek, puckers to the side and you end up kissing her on the cheek. Side kissing."

"Tha, tha, that's all she does anymore" Curt was ready to go into a full coronary.

"How's the sex life? Too busy, too tired, she's got her period again, like the fourth week in a row?" one of the drivers they called the Rock asked.

"I told her she better get to the doctor to check...Oh MY GOD, how FUCKEN STUPID AM I?" as Curt's self pity began to turn to rage.

"I think he's heard enough." Bill, now intervened on Curt's behalf. "We better get back to work."

Back to work they went, all feeling Curt's pain as they relived their own pain over again. But to each of them it helped them cope with their own loss of security. It always helped to have the image of the new guys realizing his wife is screwing everyone but him and the horrific image on their face. Plus for every new guy, people tend to forget the look they had on their face during their time of need.

Turning his head to look at the clock radio, caused a small trail of drool from the left side of his lip, onto his bed and landing across the side of his cheek and ear, like a single strand of a spider web you walked through and can't get off. The time was 9:30 and Curtis was already laying in his own self pity and spit for 45 minutes and still didn't have the energy to get back out of bed.

Curtis thought about what had gone down the week before at work. He had thought about what he could have done different to save his job, but the more he thought about it, deep down he knew the writing was already on the wall. Going back and reviewing what went down over and over in his head, Curtis knew no matter what he did, he was out at work. However, being the fall guy for something he hadn't done really bothered him. Curt was responsible for the count of "Red Bull", the drink that gives you wiings. Unfortunately, the drink gave Curt his wings right out of a job. Curt had been counting the drink and realized cases were missing on a daily basis. He passed this information on to his superiors, but it seemed to fall on a deaf ear. When Curt missed his daily count because of leaving on vacation, suddenly all hell broke loose. His superiors knew he was struggling to complete all his job functions, and was told he could avoid the count if he needed to. When Curt came back from vacation, he was suddenly questioned on the cases missing and why he suddenly missed a count just before vacation. He knew he was set up.

"You can fire me for my work ethic, you can fire me for my attitude, but God damnit, you are not going to fire me for stealing. I've been with this company over 10 years, done nothing but break my back for you, and this is how you repay me. I want you to answer one question," as he looked the overweight Vice-President square in the eyes. "Do you really think I had anything to do with the theft of the Red Bull?"

Not flinching, Rob the fat slob of a man, who recently had a mild heart attack, looked Curt right back eye to eye and said "I should have you arrested for stealing."

Curt became enraged, which was the exact reaction Rob was looking to get. Rob got his job originally because his dad was best friends with the owner of the company. He had previously worked for a trucking company and was brought in to try to break the union. He was so hated there, that his car tires were slashed, his car was keyed, people would spit in his coffee when he wasn't looking, and one guy even took a shit in the front seat of his car. Rob wasn't well liked by the employees at his current job either. Though he thought it was a nice gesture when they kept buying chicken wings and offering him as many as he wanted. Rob took them up eating 10-20 almost every day. All these union guys, had hoped to kill the fat bastard, but only a mild heart attack came from the chicken fat. Though a mild heart attack, the workers still felt elated, since it kept the fat ass out of the company for almost a month. Being union brothers who stuck together, they showered Rob with a surprise party with heavily frosted crème cake, and of course pizza and lots of wings. If the initial "surprise" didn't kill him, maybe down the road his cholesterol would.

"THAT'S ENOUGH! Rob I want to talk to you in private." Screamed Steve, Curt's immediate supervisor. Though Curt and Steve had bumped heads in the past, Steve knew what a good worker Curt is and he was tired of Rob coming down hard on Curt. Plus, he noticed the look in Curt's eye that he was one move of pounding the living shit of Rob. So off into the next office the two headed, Curt able to make out most of the conversation as Steve fought to save Curt's job. In the end, the office became quieter and the sound of silence, was not a welcome sound to Curt's ears. He knew it was over.

Steve walked in first, not making eye contact with Curt. Rob followed, stared at Curt and began to speak while still standing. "We feel it's best if we part ways." Rob proceeded to sit down. "We will give you a severance package and insurance for a month and we won't fight unemployment if you just walk away."

Curt looked over at Steve, who refused to make eye contact. He turned his head to Rob, looked him square in the face, stood up leaning all his body weight on his two hands that were balanced by his knuckles on the table, and leaned in across the table towards Rob. Rob proceeded to push his chair away from the table as he leaned as far back in it as he could, not knowing what to expect next. For a guy that could bench press over 300 lbs and not being afraid of attempting to break unions, or any one individual, Rob showed a glare of nerves by opening his eyes, not knowing what to anticipate from Curt. Curt could be the nicest guy in the world, but once he became upset; he had a look that would scare anyone. The look came from Curt attempting to hold back his frustration and anger. If he released it, watch out. Curt was wound up as tight as a garage door spring that was on the verge of snapping. From the years of hard work and the abuse taken, it was only a matter of time before the garage spring would snap sending the garage door down in a violent and uncontrollable slam to the ground. This man, calling him a thief was more than Curt could take. Rob was about to be slammed to the floor with all the force Curt could spring at him.

"Curt Schmidt, you have a call on ext 120.", the receptionist blared her message over the sound system, just enough to snap some sense back into Curt.

Curt looked at Rob and thought to himself that this fat jerk wasn't worth going to jail over. "Fuck you, asshole. You so much as bother me again, I will come back and fuck you up." Curt paused for a moment, "I don't know how you live with yourself, you may have power in this company, but you're a pathetic excuse for a man." Curt turned towards Steve "Thanks, for trying." Curt gave one more glance towards Rob, as to tell him not to say a thing or I will hurt you, before he took one step back, turned and walked out the door and headed back to his office to get a few personal items, before heading out the door for the last time.

The time now read 11:34 and all Curt had to show for his day so far was dry spit on his cheek and a crease from his ruffled bed sheet on his other cheek.

Chapter 2 Odd Companion

With all the energy Curt could muster, he slowly lifted himself up from the bed, only to flop face first back on to it. He dragged his feet to the side letting them drop to the floor, so he could attempt to get up and moving around from his depressed state of self pity. He lifted himself up grabbing the bed post as if it were actually offering him support from falling down. Curt knew he had to do something to get his mind out of a funk. He decided to work on building a storage cabinet he had previously started in the garage. He first headed to the bathroom, because even though his thoughts were to build the cabinet, needing to go to the bathroom is actually what got him to move out of bed.

So he sat, on the toilet, thinking of where and when his life went wrong. He asked God why these things were happening to him. Throughout his life, Curt never seemed to gotten a break in life. He thought about the job he thought he had in Portsmouth, New Hampshire. Just out of college, he was picked to be interviewed for an analyst position at an insurance company, whose name he could not remember now. He flew to Portsmouth, with another recent college grad, Connor, who also was vying for this position. They were both met by an unbelievably beautiful young woman, who at most was a year older than Curt. Curt could not help but be enamored with her. Sara was assigned to pick the two candidates up and get them to their hotel. When they reached the hotel, Curt asked her if there was a place to eat in town that she could recommend. Sara mentioned a seafood restaurant which was known for their cuisine. Being young, bold and confident, Curtis asked if she would like to join him for dinner. Caught off guard, this long dark haired, blue-eyed beauty lost her business composure and eye contact with the candidates, suddenly looking down, smiling, and brushing her hair with her hand, by moving her hair behind her ear. "I appreciate the offer, but I have other commitments tonight." Sara smiled as she now was making eye contact with Curtis. "However, I will be having lunch with you tomorrow, my treat; well at least the companies treat. I'll make sure both of you get checked in, and I will see you" looking directly at Curt, "tomorrow."

"I look forward to it." Curt smiled as the three began walking into the turn of the century hotel.

After Sara left, Connor turned to Curt "Man you got balls to ask her out. She might be your boss."

Curt responded, "I didn't ask her out, I just offered her to go to dinner with us. I mean, I assumed you were already going?"

"Oh yeah, not a problem. We'll just throw our luggage in our rooms and head out. I'll have the front desk get us a taxi."

So the two would be candidates headed to their rooms, which were on the second floor, Curt's room closest to the stairs, with Connor's room two rooms down.

At dinner, Curt ordered stuffed shrimp with crab meat and lobster. Connor ordered a steak. "If you don't like seafood, we could've gone somewhere else."

"Oh, I like seafood, but I don't feel like it" Connor responded back.

This struck Curt as odd, because you're in a city known for seafood, you like it, probably have one opportunity to embrace it, yet still not order it. As dinner continued, Connor went overboard to announce that he really, really, really, wanted this job. Curt felt the same, but Connor almost gave the opinion there was something more than just this job. Almost as if he was running away from something. Curt felt uncomfortable with the strange comments Connor talked about. Curt couldn't wait for dinner to be over, so he could just relax in his room and get away from this strange companion he felt obligated to be with. The taxi ride back to the hotel was just as strange. The taxi driver had a devilish view of the city and discussed how this would be one of the first cities to go in a nuclear proliferation. This seemed to excite Connor. As the two talked about the world ending, views of the shooting of President Reagan, and what it would be like to be dead, Curt was relieved to see the hotel come into view. The driver turned to collect the fare, when Connor said he was short money, forcing Curtis to pay the entire fare. It was a small price, since Curtis knew he would not have to deal with this strange character anymore. The driver, whose pointed eyebrows and devilish smile gave Curt the creeps, stated "I like that guy. I see a future for him."

Curt thought to himself "For him? What about me? That guy is nuts. Maybe he can drive taxi with you psycho." Curt pulled back a dollar from the tip.

As Curt walked away the driver blurted out, "I know what I'm talking about. I'm not psycho." He laughed as he drove away.

Curt was somewhat dumbfounded, thinking "did I say he was psycho out loud? Nah, of course a psycho wouldn't think he's psycho." Curt headed upstairs to his room.

The doors to the room were very difficult to open. You had to turn the key and the door handle at just the right angle to open the door. Curt struggled to open the door taking about 10 minutes to open. He went inside and grabbed an ice bucket and proceeded to get ice and some soda, only to then spend the next 15 minutes struggling to open the door again. Curt finally settled in, turning on the television and proceeded to watch the last episode of MASH. Disappointed with the series finale, Curt turned off the TV, and proceeded to imagine his life in this town. Closing his eyes, Curt was out cold until the phone rang for his requested 6 a.m. wake up call.

Blurry eyed, Curt stumbled out of bed gaining the exuberant feeling of a new life in a new city. With each step toward the bathroom he awakened a little more excited about his day. Curt had been on interviews before, but this was a fantastic opportunity for him. Usually, Curt would feel a bit nervous going into an interview. Today was different. Today he knew he would be the difference. Curt went to the bathroom and attempted to flush the toilet, but the toilet wouldn't flush. He took the porcelain top off the toilet and noticed there was no water pressure. He adjusted the filter float, allowing for more water to enter and to his surprise, toilet pressure. Hell, if I can fix a toilet, I can surely handle a couple of interviews today. So with a kick in his step, Curt shaved, showered, and got dressed.

Looking at the time, now 7:06, he realized he had to get moving. Sara was to pick him up at 7:30 and being late was not an option, if he was looking to make a good first impression. Curt gathered his belongings and placed them in his suitcase, because he needed to check out of the room, so the company would not be charged an additional day at the hotel. In one hand was his suitcase that he carried his pajamas, clothes he wore down and the clothes he would wear home, along with his sneakers and shoes. In his other hand was his suit coat bag, where he had kept his suit and needed to place his suit after the interviews. No way would he wear his suit after the interviews, because he would have to take an hour and a half on a bus back to the airport, then a two hour flight home. Curt struggled trying to close the door behind him using his foot to grab the bottom of the door. He was unsuccessful in fully closing the door. Curt had left the door open about 3 inches. "Oh, screw it. The maids will thank me, because they won't have to struggle opening these antiquated door locks. So downstairs he headed, knowing he was right on schedule to be in the main lobby. However, he was a little disappointed when he found out they had no vending machines to grab a quick snack. Curt just hoped that his stomach wouldn't growl during his interviews.

About 5 minutes before Sara was to pick Curt up, Connor made his way to the lobby. He was extremely agitated and nervous. Curt had never seen anybody so nervous before an interview. Plus the fact, the first interview probably wouldn't be until 9 am. "Relax, guy. Nothin' to be nervous about. Just be yourself." Curt offering what he felt was sound advice.

Connor just walked away wringing his hands together and keeping his back towards Curt. "Alrighty, then." Curt thought to himself as he noticed Sara pulling up.

He met Sara outside as she was getting out of the front of the 1983 red Caprice. "Good morning." Curt smiling, looking at how beautiful the sun shined on the head and shoulders of Sara. "I couldn't ask for a better start to the day." Curt's confidence growing with every word he spoke.

"Good morning. I hope you slept well. Are you still interested in lunch today?" Sara flirtatiously responded.

"Absolutely." Curt reacted excitedly. "Any place special we will be eating?"

"We call it the cafeteria." Sara teasingly, was able to catch Curt off guard. She looked around and asked "Where's Connor, is he ready?"

"He must still be in the lobby. Should I go get him?" Curt suggested, but then realizing Connor was just walking out the door, still nervous, as he entered the car without saying a word. Sara and Curt look at him, looked at each other, and both smiled as they shrugged their shoulders, in disbelief of the rudeness Connor just presented himself.

Connor had jumped in the back seat with sun glasses on, so Curt proceeded to sit up front with Sara, as she talked about the company, herself, and what are day would be like. Sara seemed to have it all together. She was confident, beautiful, smart, and had great legs, that she must have done a lot of aerobics. Curt thought that nothing could faze this girl. So they drove to the corporate building, neither a care in the world, with Connor in the back, with his sunglasses still on, arms folded, slouched in the backseat.

They were met by a number of candidates in the lobby. Curt didn't expect so many candidates at one time. He expected maybe two or three other candidates, but when he noticed eight or nine candidates, he knew his "A" game must be on. He knew he would be interviewing for a number of different positions, but he clearly wanted to leave his best impression. So there he sat making small talk with some of the other candidates, while waiting to be called to one of the interviews. Sara came back, with and proceeded to take one of the candidates who were involved in conversation with Curt and a couple others. "Don't worry" she smiled at them, directing the majority of her attention to Curt, "You'll all get your chance".

Everyone in the group let out a smile and nervous laugh as they waited for their chance to be interviewed. Across the lobby sitting by himself, was Connor, his elbows on his knees as he laid his chin above his crossed knuckles, sort of bobbing his head with his thumbs. He didn't look right, but nerves can do that to you. At least he had removed his sunglasses.

Time went by at it was almost 10 to 10, and no one else was sent on any interviews. Curt thought how strange it was to be sitting so long. He thought they would have been better organized in setting up the interviews. A few minutes later, Sara came back, looking nervous, and clearly lacked the confidence she had displayed previously with Curt. "It looks like she just got her ass chewed out, big time!" Curt thought to himself as he tried to make eye contact with Sara to no avail.

"Your next, Curt" Sara mumbled, never making eye contact with Curt.

Curt proceeded to pick up his resumes he had placed on the table in front of him. By the time he grabbed them, he noticed Sara was a good 15 feet away from him. He excused himself as he walked between the coffee table and other candidates and did a quick jog to catch up to Sara. Sara kept walking as Curt was forced to follow behind her. She turned a corner and only glanced back to make sure Curt had followed. She proceeded down the hall, opened a door to a conference room, now looking straight ahead like a doorman in a hotel, Curt trying to get her attention, with no luck. "Have a seat in here; someone will be right with you."

"Well I guess, I'll see you at lunch?" Curt questioned in a playful way in an attempt to break the suddenly uncomfortable feeling both were displaying.

"Change in plans. We're running behind. Good luck with your interviews." Sara never looked at Curt until she was about to walk out the door. But at the last moment before leaving, she stared at him, finally making eye contact with

him. He smiled but received no response from Sara.
"You'll be fine."

"I'll be fine? Jesus, how tough are these interviews?"   He
thought of the odd statement from Sara. "Do I look
nervous, I don't feel nervous? She must be off her game
right now. She must have really did something wrong."

As the day carried on Curt went from one interview to the
next. He interviewed with 9 different people during a total
of 7 interviews. Some of the interviews were extremely
business professional, while others were very casual.
During the casual interviews, Curt made sure not to let his
guard down. "So you rode in with Sara?" Dan a recently
married 28 year old man asked Curt"

"Yes" Curt quickly responded.

"Man, I wouldn't mind getting a piece of that ass. She is
smokin' hot. Don't you think?"

What a loaded question. Answering this could make or
break the whole interview. "She is very attractive. Her
personality really adds to her beauty." Curt directed the
response directly back to Dan, even though Russ was
interviewing Curt at the same time.

Dan and Russ looked at each other, almost stone faced
before Russ looked at Curt, smiling and laughing. "Ah, he's
just messin' with you. What we really want to know is if

you live up here, will you become a Patriots fan over a Bills fan?"

There was more to this question that shown on the surface. Were they looking for loyalty or were they looking for a kiss ass that would do and say what they wanted to hear. "I'm clearly a Buffalo Bills fan. I do like the Patriots and I do enjoy the rivalry. I think over time I could become more of a Patriot fan, but my whole life I grew up watching the Bills. I remember my dad taking me to my first game. It was incredible. Seeing the field for the first time right at the 50 yard line was an experience, I'll never forget. Plus the Bills blew out Houston 45 to 24."

"You wouldn't get fired up over another team?" Russ questioned, staring at Curtis to see what type of reaction he would get out of him.

"The Bills are my team; it will take a long time to change my feelings toward them. I believe in loyalty." Curtis suggested, hoping to get a subliminal message to his interviewers.

Little did he know that they were trying to play him, with their own subliminal messages. Curtis left the interview, feeling good, but suddenly realized they never discussed any real employment position.

After a long day, Curt was met by the ensemble of candidates back in the lobby. Everyone was discussing their interviews. "Hey how'd you do", one of the candidates asked Curt as he sat down.

"I don't know, I think I did pretty well. How did you do?" Curt replied back.

"It's tough to say. I only interviewed with 3 people. A few others had four. This guy" as the curly brown hair candidate pointed to Connor "only had two. How many did you have?"

Suddenly, feeling extremely confident, Curt leaned in and stated "I had 7 interviews!"

"Get out! Oh, you are so in!" As the curly haired kid, with a Brooklyn accent, acknowledged Curt's success.

Connor heard this and slouched back in his seat, looking defeated. "You really think so?" Curt stated as if he was trying to downplay this fact, but couldn't hide his smile.

Right then Sara showed up and everyone's attention was toward her. She still didn't seem her earlier self, but something was still clearly weighing on her mind. "Mr. Davis, the Vice-President would like to see you." Sara directed her full attention to Curtis.

Everyone was in awe of Curt. The Vice-President wanted to speak to him. You could hear the "Good job" and "Way to go" from the other candidates, except Connor who just groaned in his seat.

Curt leaped up, his chest out, shoulders back, with his head held high. He looked and felt like a proud Peacock, strutting himself. He walked next to Sara, who still didn't say much. Curt was lost on words, as he dreamed about the upcoming job offer. "I did it. I've finally proven myself." Curt thought as he walked down the hallway.

Sara knocked on Mr. Davis' door as he invited Curtis in and telling Sara to wait outside.

"So what do you think of our town?" Mr. Davis asked as he extended out his hand in a congratulatory fashion, placing his left hand on Curt's right shoulder. "Have a seat."

"It's really beautiful up here. I could really enjoy it up here."

"How was your flight? Was it okay? How about the hotel? Was it to your liking?"

"Flight was great." Curt responding to the small talk, "The hotel was nice, but the locks to try to open the door to your room, were really difficult."

"...and this frustrated you, Curt?" Mr. Davis posture changing as he sat back in his blue pinstripe suit.

"I wouldn't say frustrate, just that the locks were hard to open." Curtis sensed a change in demeanor of Mr. Davis.

"I see. Did you have any other problems with your room?"
Mr. Davis grabbing a pencil and began to play with it.

"Everything was fine." Curtis answered honestly.

"Well, I'm not going to beat around the bush anymore. "
Mr. Davis leaned in, placing the pencil horizontal to his
body, on to the desk. His elbows now down on the desk in
a folded position as he leaned ever so forward. "There
was a problem in your room."

Curt's face lit up, remembering the toilet not flushing.
When he adjusted the toilet he must have caused it to
overflow. Curt nodded as he waited for his opportunity to
clarify this problem.

"The water damage was quite extensive." Curt's face now
confused as Mr. Davis described the room. "The water
from the sprinkler system damaged a number of rooms.
"Do you smoke?"

"Huh?" Curt was confused that this wasn't about the
toilet. Sprinkler systems and does he smoke, just wasn't
registering in his head. "I don't smoke. Why do y...."

"There was a fire at the hotel."

Curt now understood. His luggage must have been burned
in the fire. "Oh, my God. I hope everyone is okay?"

"Everyone's fine."

"Oh good. Then I'm guessing my luggage was lost in the fire? There wasn't anything that can be repl…"

Mr. Davis cut off Curtis to explain "The fire started in your room. The fire investigators went in after the fire was extinguished and said the fire started in your room. I guess they are able to tell by darkness of the ceiling."

"I don't smoke. I don't carry a lighter or matches. Why would I want to start a fire?" Curtis now leaning forward his head down, but rose just long enough to speak to Mr. Davis. "I didn't start any fire." Curt's voice cracking as the thoughts ran through his mind. "They think I started this." He thought. "They weren't interviewing me all day, they were interrogating me. I'm so humiliated. Oh, God. I have to face all those people out there. Sara she must think I'm an arsonist. No wonder she was acting so strangely. How am I going to explain this to my parents? The police are going to call them. THEY'RE GOING TO ARREST ME! I didn't do anything….I left that damn door open. Are you fuckin' kidding me! I'm going to jail because I left a fucking door open." Curt's hands over his head in disbelief, trying to hold back tears.

Mr. Davis stood up walked around his desk and sat on the corner directly in front of Curt. "You have to go back to the hotel to get your items. The way the fireman described how it was left, they don't think you did it. Someone knew what they were doing. Just one question, how do you think they got in your room?"

"The locks...I had trouble with opening the locks. I...., I left the door open a little, so the maids didn't have to struggle opening the door." Curtis looked at Mr. Davis like a beaten puppy, who did nothing wrong , but be in the way of an angry man.

"Sara will take you back to the hotel. You can get your things and go home. Don't worry, everything will be okay." With that advice, Mr. Davis opened the door having Sara come just inside the doorway. "You can go now."

Curtis stood up, but never lifted his eyes off the ground, embarrassed on how these people thought of him. Mr. Davis shook his hand, and stated sincerely if he needed anything to call him, as he handed Curtis his card.

"Thank you" barely an audible mumble came out of Curt's mouth.

Sara walked next to Curt slowly, as if he just had major surgery, and needed someone to catch him if his knees were to give out. Curt's shoulders were slumped, his head hanging, a complete 180 of the entrance into Mr. Davis' office. Sara had him sit down, telling all the other candidates, expressing concern and curiosity to leave him alone. "I'll be right back with the car." Sara placed her hands on Curt's shoulder and giving a slight squeeze. Deep down she knew this wasn't his fault.

After Sara left, everyone was asking Curt what was going on. Curt never looked up at them. What could he say? That he was possibly being blamed for being an arsonist. That he is probably on his way to jail? Hell, worse yet, they probably already knew. Curt got up and walked toward the doorway to wait for Sara. Connor jumped up, quizzing Curt on what was going on. Curt just ignored him.

Sara pulled up with her car. Curt proceeded this time directly to the back seat. Connor jumped in the front seat. "C'mon, c'mon, what's going on" as the adrenaline seemed to suddenly flow through his veins.

"None of your business," Curt was grinding his teeth as he growled at Connor.

"He is only going to find out when we get back to the hotel," Sara interrupted and began to tell Connor what happened.

Curt now was the one slouched in the back seat. His arms crossed and looking out the window, he dreaded going back to the hotel. Connor was gleeful, cracking jokes and making conversation like he hadn't before. Sara just drove not saying a word. Curt anticipated being arrested and was preparing himself for that.

Finally, after an eternity of a car ride, they were back at the hotel. Black smoke had dyed the outside of the white building, marking the windows where Curt's room was.

They were met by a fire investigator. A policeman was also there, but did not greet the three arrivals.

Connor jumped out of the car stating "Sorry, you're not looking for Me." pointing to the backseat of the car where Curt was getting out.

Not amused the fire investigator snapped "Then I guess it's none of your business. I suggest you stay out of the way." Glaring at Connor, as Connor put his hands up in a surrender motion and turned and walked toward the hotel lobby, snickering under his breath. "Are you Curtis Schmidt?" looking directly at Curtis. "I'm fire investigator Seymour. Let's take a walk and see what happened."

Sara stood at the front of the car "I'll wait here until you come back," Showing emotion in her voice as she knew in her heart that this was not Curt's fault.

"HEY! WAIT FOR ME!" The overweight manager with dandruff on his shoulders from his greasy, graying hair waddled up from the lobby, pointing his finger at Curtis. "I want to hear what he has to say for himself. I'm Mike Danieu and I run this hotel." He was out of breath as he approached the two men.

The police officer stood up from leaning on his vehicle as the obnoxious manager approached the others. He was prepared to intervene, but soon relaxed when investigator Seymour stopped the manager in his tracks. "I'm going to tell you once, keep your mouth shut. If you hinder this investigation at all, I'll have you arrested."

Hearing this, Curt was prepared to be arrested. He decided that he wasn't going to be afraid, but decided that he was the only one who was going to stand up for his rights. He would be honest and was prepared to tell the truth, even if it meant he would be in trouble for the leaving the door open. The three headed toward the stairs to the second floor, with Danieu puffing ahead, and the other two following a few steps back.

When Curt entered the room Mike Danieu was standing in the middle of it, cursing under his breath. Curt did not expect what he witnessed. There he saw the mattresses from both beds were both pushed into the middle of the floor, burned completely to the floorboards and the ceiling completely charred above the mattresses. The whole roomed was blackened from the soot caused from the fire. All the ashes they stepped on were still wet from the water system and help from the fireman.

"They had to evacuate 42 people. You could have killed 42 people, you Son of a bitch!" growled Danieu as he became angrier and angrier every time he looked at the damage.

"I didn't do this. What the hell is wrong with you? Why would I possibly want to do this?" Curtis snapped back. He felt like he was trapped in a corner.

"Oh I don't know. Maybe, because you're a sick asshole."
Danieu walked towards Curt.

Curt leaned forward, not giving an inch of room to the
bitter manager who rolled towards him. "I didn't do this
you fat fuck…"

"THAT'S ENOUGH. KNOCK IT OFF" Seymour screamed out
as he pulled Curt back, placing himself between the two. "I
told you to keep your mouth shut!" He Looked directly at
Danieu. He turned back toward Curt, "Explained to me
what happened. Do you smoke?"

"No, I don't smoke. I don't know what happ…."

"YOU JUST MOVED THE MATTRESSES TOGETHER AND LIT
THEM" Danieu interjected trying to push the issue.

"I just said I don't smoke. What would I light them with? I
have no need to carry a lighter." Curt's voice, now
becoming visibly shaken.

"There are only complimentary matches, in every room."
Danieu stated as if he just caught a Columbo moment of
AHHHA in solving the case.

"Then I suggest you not leave them in every room. It looks
to me like it's a pretty bad idea." Curt's voice shouted
down the notion that Danieu even had a glimpse of a
correct thought. "I didn't even know you left matches in
the room." Curtis stated confidently back at the raging
bull.

"I've heard enough" Seymour putting his head down, shaking it in disbelief. "You stay here. If you come down those stairs, I'll have you arrested, I'm very serious. I'll come back for you. "His finger pointed at Danieu and eyeballing him, letting him know, he wasn't screwing with him. "Curtis, go downstairs and wait for me," as he never took his eyes off Danieu.

Curt headed down the stairs, not knowing where to go. He looked over at Sara, who was still waiting by her car. Behind her he could see Connor had already changed into jeans. He leaned on a lamp post, one foot on the pole, his right foot on the ground, with his back leaning against it. Curtis looked directly at Connor and deep down Curtis felt he knew who did this. Connor stood against the pole, sunglasses on, but Curtis could see through the shades at Connor's soul. He knew Connor did this. It made sense. Connor discussed how badly he wanted this job that was beyond normalcy. His nervousness and lack of eye contact when he came down this morning. His eagerness to know what was going on. He had a sudden happiness and cockiness, when Curt was in trouble. Curt thought about telling Seymour, but he knew he couldn't. I f he had started pointing fingers, Curt would have made himself look guilty. There Connor stood, smug as could be, knowing he was about to get away with arson.

"LETS talk" Seymour startling Curtis, as he had come down the stairs. "Tell me now, what happened this morning. I want to know when you got up, brushed your teeth, combed your hair, up until you left the room."

In detail Curt discussed everything, including the problem with the toilet, up until his fateful mistake of trying to do a favor by leaving the door partially opened. When Curt was done, he figured he probably shouldn't have said so much. Now they can poke holes in his story. Seymour walked over to the officer still waiting by his car. They spoke out of range for about five minutes, with the officer periodically looking over at Curtis, before he turned to open his car door, to enter and eventually leave. Seymour had walked back to where Curt was standing, almost frozen in place. "it's time to go."

Curt looked confused as the police car was already pulling out of the hotel. Sara walked over towards to two men, to find out what was going on. "Gather your things, before you miss your bus back to the airport." Inspector Seymour turned his attention to Sara. "Give this kid a ride. He's had a pretty tough day. Now I still have to deal with the almighty upstairs. I want you gone before that manager goes ballistic on me. I have your name and number, I'll be in touch."

Curtis never heard from him again. Nor did he receive any job offers. He just went on his first trip through hell.

Curt wiped his ass, flushed a working toilet, and washed his hands, as more and more of his past memories ran through his head. He looked at the clock and seen it was about 10 to 12. He went back in his room and got dressed. He walked out and stared at the photos of his mom on the wall. He really missed her. It was 15 years since she died, but it seemed like yesterday that he held her in his arms for the last time...

Chapter 3 Oh, My Mama, To Me She Is So Beautiful

Curt's mom had died of lung cancer. She died before she ever met his children. June would have loved his children. June was a beautiful woman with curly dark hair that she had to dye to keep it her auburn color. Her curls were the work of prickly curlers that she slept in so she could have her curly rings in the morning. Curt remembered how his mom would wake up early each day. She loved the peacefulness of the mornings. She enjoyed the sounds of the birds flying outside the kitchen window. Every morning she would sit with her feet up on the chair, her shins pressing into the side of the table, causing a deep crease in her leg, just below her knees. June would listen to the sounds of silence and enjoy her cup of coffee and unfortunately her cigarettes.

Curt would wake up as a small boy and his mother always greeted him with a smile and a "good morning, honey." No matter what her mood may have been, she always greeted Curt with a smile. This smile was the one thing that always seemed to keep Curt going. Curt always wore his heart on his sleeve, never fearing what people thought of his emotions. He would have been happier had he not always shown his emotions. His mother hid her emotions very well. Curt could always tell when his mom was hurting inside. He hated knowing this. June would always downplay whatever was bothering her, but Curt always could figure it out. He had a bond with his mom that he thought would never be broken.

Curt remembered what his mother told him during one of his last conversations, before she became too ill to speak. Curt had kissed his mom and told her he loved her as he hugged her frail body that was less than 100 lbs. Her arms were as thin as her wrist, as the cancer had completely taken her appetite away. "I love you too." She said in a proud voice that Curt was her grown man, but in a way, always would be her baby son. "Someday, you will understand what it is like to love a child. You think you love me," as June addressed the closeness the two had always shared, "but the love of your child, nothing will ever compare to it. You love me. You love your father, your fiancé, and your family and friends. Wait until your child is born. You will never know what true love is until you hold your child for the first time. You remind me, son, of my own dad. He had the same personality as you and did I love that man. He was a wonderful person and a wonderful dad. I never thought I could love another person the way I loved him. Then you were born and I couldn't believe the love I felt for you. I had felt pure love from my dad and only experienced pure love when I held you. Wait until you hold your children. You will finally understand the meaning of God's love."

Tears were rolling down Curt's eyes, as began to cry uncontrollably. He understood what his conversation was about. June held her son in her arms and spoke softly in his ear. "I hope I've been a good mom to you." Curt nodded with his head still pressed on June's shoulder. "It's okay to cry for me now, but I want you to grow up happy and enjoy life. You promise?" Curt again nodded. "I just needed to tell you how much I love you, because I don't have very long left on this earth. I needed to tell you Good-bye. I love you and thank God for you every day."

September came and Curt was taking care of his mother, who now lay motionless in bed. The oxygen mask was consistently on helping with her shallow breathes. Curt's dad, Bill, who was also named after his father, stood at the end of the bed and placed his hands on the top of June's feet. "I'm going out to get a haircut." His voice started to crack "I'll be right back. I just want you to know how proud I am of how hard you fought this disease. I know you fought hard for me and the kids, but it's okay if you to stop fighting now. I love you very much. I've always had and always will." He walked around the bed and kissed his wife on her forehead. His eyes clutched closed in disbelief that his life with his wife of 40 years was almost over. He lightly rubbed the back of his hand on June's temple down to her upper cheek, being stopped by the oxygen mask that was sustaining her breathing. He looked at his son, smiled and turned back to his wife and kissed her on her forehead again. As he walked back down to the end of the bed, Bill Jr. gently grabbed his wife's feet with his hands, leaned over and kissed the top of her feet, showing his honor and respect for his longtime bride. "You did well, really, really, well." He had given his wife his blessing for the first time since they found out about her cancer.

Curt walked around the bed to the other side and crawled in carefully, as he had done when he was a little boy. He made every effort not to cause any abrupt movements that would cause additional pain to his mom. He lay next to her and held her hand, as he touched his head against hers. He closed his eyes and thought about their life together. Curt thought how lucky he was to have such a beautiful woman, the most beautiful person, be his mom. His friends admired and respected her as much, if not more than their own parents. Anyone who ever met June loved June.

Curt thought about the time he was nine. Curt was in the backseat with his mom, his grandmother sitting next to them. Bill was driving and Bill Sr., his grandfather, sat in the front passenger seat. They were coming back from a Christmas concert and Carly Simon's song You're So Vain was on the radio. Curt didn't know if it was the music on the radio, or coming back from the Christmas concert, or the holiday season, but with his head on his mom's lap, he never felt more secure, relaxed, and loved. Curt twisted his head to look up at his mom, as she was caressing his hair and she looked down in a way only a parent could. In her eyes and smile, he felt a love ever so pure. Curt smiled, closed his eyes, and listened to the radio. To this day, whenever he listens to <u>You're So Vain,</u> he is brought back to that moment back in the early 1970's.

Curt wanted to hug his mother, but couldn't because of her frailty. Curt closed his eyes, which seemed for just a moment, and he found himself in a dream state. Curt found himself with his mom in a completely white room. The room had no doors or windows. The room didn't have furniture nor were there even corners in the room. It was if Curt and his mom were the only ones who existed in the universe. There his mom stood across from Curt. She stared directly into his eyes. Curt noticed his mom was no longer ill. She was the beautiful and vibrant woman who raised him. She took a small step toward Curt and asked, "I have to die now...don't I?"

Curt wanted to tell her how proud he was of her and that he no longer wanted to see her suffer anymore. He wanted to tell her how much she was loved and how he especially loved her and would never forget her. However, like a frightened child, he instead dropped his head in shame and mumbled "yes."

June held her son's hands and told him, "It's Okay." She lifted her right hand and placed it under Curt's chin to lift it, so she could again look at him eye to eye. Curt looked at her, and she gave him a reassuring smile, letting him know everything would be okay. At that moment, Curt felt a rush of love, like the feeling he felt over 20 years earlier. June squeezed his hand and with a smile, Curt was awakened.

Curt looked down at their holding hands, when he noticed his mom squeezing his hand. Curt kissed her on the forehead and said, "I love you, too."

As Curt stared at his mom, he noticed an ever slight change in her breathing. For whatever reason, Curt knew his mom's time had come. No longer the frightened child, he proceeded to tell his mom, "Mom, we love you. Everyone is going to miss you so much. You have made me so happy. You are the best mom a kid could ever ask for. I will never forget you. I love you, so, so, much. You did a great job raising us kids and I know how much dad is going to miss you. None of us will ever, meet anyone who is as wonderful of you. God, I love you mom." Curt talked and talked until he felt comfortable that his mom was no longer there in body or spirit.

Curt made the appropriate phone calls, including calls to his siblings. After Curt hung up, with his last call, the door opened. His dad walked in, and Curt looked at him and his dad knew. They hugged and proceeded to enter the bedroom together.

Curt had a feeling that his mom's death was scripted by God. His dad left for just a short time and Curt was able to spend one last time with his mom. Curt comforted his mom until he felt okay to leave the room. He made phone calls and then his father walked back into the house. Curt knew he would need to spend time consoling his dad. This was too coincidental. The timing was too perfect. This must have been scripted by God. This was either divine intervention, or like a good mom, she held his hands until the end. Maybe it was a little of both. Curt believed in God, but wasn't religious. However, it struck him odd that his father had left for a short time. His mom knew that his dad would not have handled her dying on his watch. Out of all the siblings, Curt would have been his mom's choice to be there when she died. She didn't favor him over his brother and sisters, but his brother had young children, his one sister wouldn't have handled it well, and his other sister, well, just wasn't reliable.

Curt placed his hand on the picture of his parents kissing, mourning their loss more every day. Bill Jr. had died a little over a year later of a broken heart. Curt wished just for one more day with them.

Chapter 4 The Argument

Curt headed toward the garage to finish building the cabinet. He reached for the cordless drill and attempted to use it, when he realized the battery was not charged. Curt then headed downstairs to get the electric drill, and banged his head on the corner of the furnace duct. Even though he knew he had to duck, for whatever reason, he seemed to bang his head on the corner consistently. "Mother fu...." Curt was pissed as this time he drew blood. "Can't you ever let me get something without banging my head?" Curt's eyes looked up as if he was yelling at God, as if it was his fault for his own clumsiness.

Angrily grabbing the electric drill, he headed back upstairs with the electric cord dragging behind. As he made the turn and was halfway up the stairs, the cord caught the corner of the bottom step, enough to stop Curt dead in his tracks. "What the...C'mon already".   Back down the stairs he went, to attempt to unwedge the cord, which had perfectly driven into the only spot that Curt could not get his fingers to reach. After a moment of trying to finesse out the plug, Curt thought he had it, but yanked too hard, as half the cord tore, exposing the wires. Seeing that, he yanked the cord with full force. With a sudden ease the cord came out striking Curt at the exact spot of his earlier accident from the heat duct. "ARE YOU KIDDING ME", Curt screamed at the top of his lungs, as nothing was going right. "I ask you God, for just one day, not to screw with me. Why do you have to screw with me every Goddamn day?"

Curt proceeded back upstairs leaving the drill on the table next to the bottom of the stairs. Mumbling under his breath up the stairs, he flopped his body onto the couch and put the television on, only to realize the cable was out. Curt's blood pressure grew as his face turned beet red. He was about to explode in anger, when his cell phone rang. "Hello? Oh Ms. Veranda. I can't help you with your order. Please don't scream at me. Listen," Curt paused as the one account who was nothing but a headache to him at his, job called him on his Droid. She had gotten the number when the one receptionist inadvertently gave it out in error. "Listen, Can I..., will you let me sp...." Curt was being interrupted every time he attempted to speak. "You want your order call the company, I don't .... No, no I don't know where your order is." Giving up on telling her he no longer worked for the company. "I'll make sure it will be there by the end of the day. Are you kidding me lady? You want the order within the hour? I just said I will get it to you by the end of the day. C'mon give me a fucking break." As Curt's patience with this obnoxious customer came to a climax. "What? You don't like that language? How about this then? Screw you. That's right, screw YOU. Screw you and your business as I don't care if

you even get an order. Oh you're going to tell my boss?
Go right the fuck ahead…. And while you're at it, tell him
to fuck himself too!" Curt disconnected the call in
disbelief. Even though he no longer worked for Buy It Now
Distributors, he would have called in the order to his old
boss and let him explain to this asshole customer, that he
no longer worked for the company and she shouldn't call
him anymore.   But she pushed one too many buttons and
he lost complete control with her.

"Hello" as Curt answered his phone again, first observing
that it wasn't Veranda again. "Hey, Joe." As Curt realized
it was his old supervisor. Ms. Veranda had wasted no time
calling the company, and Joe was livid the way Curt had
treated a customer. "Don't tell me what the hell to do.
Oh really, you're going after my unemployment, because
the way I spoke to your customer. You know what, I tried
to… Shut the fuck up and listen to me asshole. Yeah that's
right asshole. Why I should explain myself to you is a
waste of breath, but I will because I don't play fuckin'
games like you dickwads. SHUT UP AND LISTEN. LISTEN I
SAID! I told that bitch I would get her order to her by the
end of the day and she starts rippin' me apart like it's my
fault she hadn't received her order. I tried to explain to
her that I no longer work for you assholes, but she
wouldn't let me get a word in edgewise. So I figured I'd
make sure she received her order by the end of the day,
because I wouldn't want to burden you by rushing the
order out quicker," as the sarcasm flowed from Curt's lips.

"I was going to call you to place the order, then have youuuu explain to her not to call me anymore. But it wasn't good enough for her. She started tearing me a new asshole, so I fuckin lost it with her and told her to go screw herself. Yeah she mentioned she was going to call you, so I told her tell him to fuck himself too. Hey do what you have to do with the unemployment, I don't give a shit. That's right my attitude stinks. Let's see how you are after getting made a scapegoat and fired. Until then, go take a flying fuck, you fuck." Curt was swearing more and more as if somehow that was giving him control of the situation, when actually he had completely lost it.

Throwing his phone on the couch, he slumped on to the couch himself and began his talk with God. "Are you kidding me? So I lost it. Who gives a shit. Obviously you don't!" Curt looked up at his ceiling as if he were making eye to eye contact with God. "Why do you keep pushing me down? Isn't it bad enough every time things start looking up, you knock me down? Why? Why in the hell would you keep doing this to me? What, I don't go to church and right away you treat me like garbage? Doesn't believing in you enough? Anyhow, why do you blame me? I didn't stop going to church, my parents stopped sending me. Jesus, I was 5 years old. Every Sunday the bus would pick us up for Sunday school and every week I was told to sit next to the red headed girl Tina. Every week the older kids, including my brother and sisters, would tease us. OOOhh you two are boyfriend and girlfriend. They would embarrass us. I remember turning to Tina and telling her don't let them bug us. I tried to reassure this little girl, and she turned and just looked out the window. I tried to comfort her and she ignored me, like I was the problem. But I tolerated it, week after week, month after month, year after... okay, I don't remember how long exactly, I was FIVE! But the point is I tolerated! Why? Huh? Why? For you that's why. If you recall the last time I went to church, MY mother put me in that stupid suit. Remember, that suit? I do. It was a gray checkered suit, with matching shorts and cap. Even at five, I knew I couldn't be seen in that outfit. I would have been belittled even more. I remember the bus coming and I wouldn't go. My father grabbed my arm, and spanked me hard. But the pain from the spanking was less than the pain of embarrassment I would have had to endure. He spanked again, real hard, because I wouldn't go. I remember, my father started yelling at my mother, if he doesn't want to go, let him stay home. I'm not going to fight with this little pisspot every week. So there I sat, on the couch, crying, hurting, all because I was tired of being humiliated. Every week, I was ready to go to church, but my father wouldn't send me. I WANTED TO GO. But it became easier just to watch TV on Sunday. I swear I must have watched Jason and the Argonauts on a thousand different Sunday's. So are you pissed that I stopped trying to go to church? I never stopped believing and I constantly talked to you, yet, my life became more and more miserable. When the kids were born, I started taking them to church, because I felt it was important. But you didn't want me there. I could sense it. I felt it. I felt the cold breeze across the back of my neck, man that's not right. I know you didn't want me there. I recall a February day a few years before taking my kids to church. I was mourning over my mother's grave. The temperature outside was about 10 degrees. Yet the sun shined directly on my back and my mother's stone. Only her stone did the sun shine on that day. For over an hour I stood out there warm and comforted, in this bitter cold. Why the mixed signals? Answer me God Damnit. Or just damnit, whatever."

Curtis was breathing hard, his face flushed in anger. A man so incensed by being alone. He wondered why he was a man with such a good heart, yet everyone and everything seemed to go against him. Curt sat up, placing his head down, with his elbows on his knees and his palms of his hands on the tip of his ears, as he locked his fingers behind his head, squeezing the back of his head, as if he were trying to pop a pimple, to relieve the pressure he felt in his head. A drop of blood dripped from his forehead, somehow navigating away from his arms, missing his legs, and dripping perfectly on his white carpet.

"You got to be kidding me, right?" Curt began his conversation with the Almighty again.

Curt headed into the small half bath that was off his kitchen and grabbed some toilet paper and wiped his head. He cleared the blood, but if formed a droplet again.

Curt had given himself a pretty good gash on the top of his head. Not enough for stitches, but enough to force him to hold toilet paper balled up, to help the blood coagulate.

Curt then grabbed a rag, placed some soap and water on it and headed back to the family room to clean up his blood. With one hand holding the toilet paper over his head and the other hand holding the dripping washcloth, he turned to leave the bathroom, catching his baby toe on his left foot on the corner of the door. This time he didn't just stub it, he heard a crack like a chicken bone. The pain was excruciating as was the sound. Dropping the washcloth, he lifted his left foot and balanced on his right foot, holding his left foot up with both his hands. The bloodied toilet paper stuck to his hand as he squeezed his foot, attempting to make the throbbing pain stop. "What the hell is wrong with you, leave me the hell alone." Curt began talking again. Curt let go of his throbbing foot as he put it down on the floor, heal first, leaving his toes dangling in the air. He head outside to get some duct tape to wrap his end two toes together. "I want nothing more to do with you. You never have given me a break in life and I'm sick of it. Go screw yourself". With that Curt grabbed a deep breath and spit into the air as if to be spitting at God. "WE ARE DONE!"

Curt turned in the garage toward the duct tape, hitting a piece of wood on the floor with his baby toe. He screamed in pain, again lifting his foot to hold, while a droplet of blood and sweat, dripped into his eye burning, as he clutched it closed, attempting to wipe it on his shoulder. As he thrust his head to the side, still standing on one foot, he lost his balance and fell backwards toward the cabinet he was building, striking the back of his head hard. Curt was knocked unconscious and bleeding from the skull. Curt landed on two 2x4's that were perpendicular underneath him. Curt's arms which were held close to his body during his dance of pain, now were straight out as he had attempted to catch himself, before hitting his head. Curt lay on the wood as if he had just been crucified on the cross.

Chapter 5 Christmas Comes Early

Curt's eyes opened wide wondering what had just happened to him. He lay on the ground, trying to collect his thoughts. "Man what happened?" as he rolled onto his left side as he pushed himself up, leaving himself sitting down on the cold hard floor. He cracked his head hard on the concrete, but he felt no pain as he grabbed his head to see where the injury was. His cut on his head wasn't bleeding, so he felt he must have knocked himself out for awhile.

Slowly he stood up, forgetting about his broken toe for a split moment, before realizing how much pressure he placed on his foot. But again, he felt no pain. As he looked at his foot he noticed the concrete was painted gray. "What the...." As Curt tried to gather his thoughts "How'd I get here?"

Curt had found himself back in his basement. "I must have attempted to get myself in the house and gotten really confused." Curt thought to himself. "I've must have collapsed, down here again".

"So weird, this is bizarre" Curt speaking out still trying to comprehend exactly how he ended up back in the basement, but having no recollection on how he got there.

Curt began rubbing the back of his head ever so slightly, but felt no pain, so he rubbed harder and harder, but still no pain. He tapped, and then lightly slapped the back of his head, attempting to see if he would get some sort of migraine from the fall, but still nothing. That's when he noticed that he was standing at the bottom of his basement steps, next to the workbenches he built for storage, but realized he wasn't in his basement at all.

Somehow he was in his parent's basement. It had been years since he had been in it. The basement wasn't exactly how he remembered it. There was a corner around the one side, like the basement he remembered from his boyhood. That is when Curt's vision, finally was aware of his surroundings. The basement was like a combination of his childhood house and his parent's last house.

Curt looked to his left and he was thrown back to his childhood. There was the black three piece, sectional with the black end tables, that he used to play with his G.I. Joe Space Capsule on, using the couch as the moon surface. He remembered how the couch had almost a crater style cushion on it. On the end tables were the orange, oblique style lamps that looked as if it the black circle in the center was stretched to look like galaxies. They actually looked like ceramic lava lamps. "This is so cool. I haven't thought about this couch in years. God, these lamps sure do bring back memories"! Curt began talking aloud in his astonishment of his surroundings. Then a realization hit him "Oh, God. I'm...."

"Dead".

Curt turned to see who finished his sentence. There stood his Uncle, strong and vibrant, long before age had sucked most of the life out of him. "I didn't know you died?" Curt responded in shock. "I realize I lost touch after mom and dad died, but when..."

"I'm not dead, well I don't think I'm dead, but thanks for wishing that on me. It's Nice to see you too." Curt's Uncle Paul snapped back. "Believe it or not, I think I'm dreaming this, but you are actually dead. I was brought in to be a quick tour guide, to let you know which way you need to head." Paul was a strong, wide shoulder man, who seem to tower over Curt, even though his Uncle was only an inch and a half taller. "When I wake up, I'll remember you in my dream, but won't remember why. I'll feel melancholy, having not seen you for a long time. Glad you could take time to visit your Uncle." Paul was getting more sarcastic in his tone of voice.

"Sor-ree. Can you cut me a little slack; I am dead for Christ sake!" Curt suddenly thinking about his choice of words, using the lords name in vain.

"True. So True. And after I give you this tour, I'll wake up an old man. That sucks, considering how damn good looking I was in my youth. I got any woman at anytime I wanted. Plus being a cop didn't hurt. I remember the one time I was drivin..."

"Don't you have to wake up soon? I mean it's great seeing you and all, but what gives?"

"Look at this white Monroe style couch. Your parents had it upstairs in their house. Remember, the carpeting? You would walk across it and give out an electrical shock? Man, did decorating come a long way from the sixties. But I digress. Over here is the orange flower couch your parents had when you were in your teens. Over there is the ugly colonial one with the wooden armrest from your preteens. All the way to the back is the light blue and white couch, which was the last one your parents owned. Oh, and to the far, far, right is the golden velour style couch that your mother kept plastic on. Thank God, I told her to get rid of that one." Paul showed some pride in this fact.

"Hey, isn't that the couch my parents gave you. I remember the plastic over it at our house, but I remember the worn out velour armrests at your house."

"I know, I thought it looked better in my house too." Paul smiled a shitty grin and began to laugh when he thought about how he talked Curt's parents out of the couch. A tear from laughing began to roll from his left eye and Paul wiped it with the top of his wrist.

Curt wasn't smiling. Curt was more confused. "So why do I have to look at every couch my parent's owned?"

"Not every couch, but all their furniture." Paul waved his arms around as if he were Carol Marole from Let's Make a Deal.

Suddenly, there it all was. Every table, lamp, bed, couch, and even a portable fireplace were in front of Curt. Some of the Oriental furniture that was in Curt's home that was passed down to him was in front of him. "Why? Why all the furniture"?

"This is to prove to you that it doesn't matter. All this furniture," Paul stepping onto a maple wood coffee table;" just doesn't matter. It's all materialistic. Whether your parents were rich or poor, none of it matters now. Billionaires come here and realize how shallow they were; thinking somehow having more than another, made them a better person. Nope, it only made them materialistic." Paul looking straight faced for the first time, "All our wants in life, only a small portion matters."

"But you're like the most materialistic person I know. You always had to have the best of everything, from clothes, to food, to wine, to women. All except for that couch. What were you thinking?" Curt showed a somewhat disgusted look on his face.

"I am, and always will be, a very materialistic person. Ironic, huh? I guess that's why I'm here. Whoa, talk about killing two birds with one stone..."

They both were silent as they looked around the room, before their eyes connected to each other again. "You need to enter that room, as Paul pointed out a door at the top of three steps. I have no idea what's inside, other than more materialistic stuff. I guess I have to wait my turn. You have to go now."

Curt walked over to his Uncle, shook his hand, as his Uncle grabbed his left arm and gave him a less than enthusiastic hug. "Sorry" Paul looking put out. "I can't help thinking I'm next to go. This sucks, because I got such a great life."

"I'll see ya Uncle Paul, soon, real soon." As Curt wanted to know that where ever he was now, his Uncle would be no better than him. Curt headed up the three stairs, paused for a moment, took a deep breath and opened the door to a place of unbelievable beauty. As the door closed behind him, a feeling of comfort overwhelmed Curt.

Curt grabbed the door before it shut, turned back toward his Uncle and said "Uncle Paul you really gotta see this!" But his Uncle was gone. So was all the furniture. The basement was completely empty. Curt turned back, thinking as he turned, that the beauty he seen would be gone. Thank God, it wasn't.

Curt walked a few steps into the room and he couldn't believe his eyes. Christmas trees full of beautiful colored lights lit up the room. A white carpeted rug formed a straight path for him to walk on. The bulbs on the tree were the same ones that were on his tree as a kid. The only difference was, they were all new. He could make out his likeness, with the same distortion of his face, in each of the bulbs. The different red, blue, yellow, and green lights shone so evenly throughout each tree, and they all were so vibrant. Curt turned to his left as he heard the sound of the rubbing foil from a colored wheel that turned giving a different coloring to the tree. The sound reminded Curt of his Christmas as a boy when he received a fire truck that he was able to drive around in. He remembered how perfectly his feet reached the pedals, in his footy pajamas. He thought of the ladders that were on the side of the truck and the fire bell in front. Finally, he remembered the plastic fire helmet that he used to wear pedaling the truck around.

He admired the tree and that Christmas. Curt had completely forgot about that Christmas, but now remembered every toy he received that year, including the stuffed dog, that laid on his bed until he was a teenager. He thought about the black velvet eyes that fell off, so his mom sewed on buttons. He remembered the red tongue that stuck out of the yellow and black shaggy dog. That was the year he had made an angel that had his school picture on, that his mom immediately used as the angel on top of the tree ornament for years. Curt looked up and there it was. The cone shaped construction paper, holding a round ball of Styrofoam, with his picture glued to it, stood out on the tree. The perfect doily wings and the red pipe cleaner shaped as a halo, stood out from the silver and gold sprinkles held on by a strip of Elmer's glue. Curt remembered the look of pride his mother had shown, when he presented it to her. He walked in the front door of their home, so excited that he forgot to take off his snowy, wet boots and dragged snow from the foyer, through the living room, up into the kitchen, before his mom stopped him. His mom didn't yell because she could see the excitement in Curt's face. Curt had carried the angel home in a Wonderbread plastic bag that he took out of his boot, to protect it from getting wet. He didn't want to put it in his pocket, because he knew it would have gotten smashed. So he carried it home, keeping his hands in front of him, making it difficult to walk through the heavy snow. A couple of close calls occurred, when he walked into snow up to his waist and he fell trying to get through it. He was snow covered, but the plastic bag covering the angel only had light snow on it, that was mainly from the falling snow in the sky. Curt felt the pain of the ice cold snow getting inside his gloves and some up his coat sleeve. He knew he couldn't brush the snow out, without putting down the angel, so he had to bear with the pain. His left boot was full of snow, and his foot was soaked from not having the plastic bag covering his sock.

So as he stood there smiling from ear to ear, his hands still out straight, he handed the plastic bag to his mother. She glanced down at the melting snow on her freshly waxed floor, but never said a word to Curt. When she opened the bag, her acknowledgement of the gift was as if she was a child herself, and just received the greatest gift of all time. Her uncontrollable excitement came not from the gift, but from the pure energy of love that this woman felt for this child and this child for his mom. She hugged him and squeezed him, the whole time she held the angel behind him. Curt's mom grabbed his hand with her free hand and walked him to the Christmas tree. She handed the angel back to Curt, as she rushed back into the kitchen to grab a chair. She climbed on the chair, carefully taking the angel from Curt, telling him "Thank you honey. This is the greatest gift mommy has ever gotten", as she placed the angel on top of the tree. "This angel will always be my most favorite gift".

As Curt was reminded of this memory, he noticed all the colored lights on the trees were now all white. All the ornaments were now crystal and the top of each tree was a star. As he watched the stars, they began to emit light. A light so bright, but Curt couldn't turn away. The light seemed to fly from tree to tree. Christmas music of Andy Williams singing Happy Holidays could be heard. Curt was focused on these lights as he walked further and further into the room. The lights were angels somehow guiding him to the back of the room. There was another door, that didn't look inviting to enter. However, Curt knew these angels were guiding him to it. As Curt grabbed the door handle, a shriek was heard that went right down Curt's spine and the angels seemed to shudder and hide within the Christmas trees. Whatever, was behind the door, couldn't be good. Curt somehow knew he had to move on. Hesitantly, he opened the door and he was immediately forced in.

Chapter 6 Behind Door Number Two...

Curt's body was jarred when the door slammed behind him. He looked out at an unlighted basement, and looked at a rusted washer and dryer in the corner, the dank furnace near the back wall. Coming from the furnace were what looked like black puffs of smoke.   As they drew near Curt, they seem to pick up speed as if a flying fist was coming right at him. He tilted his head as he stepped to the side to avoid the first one. He jumped back to twisting his body, flailing his hands in an effort to avoid the second. However, there were too many and too fast for him to avoid. His body was smashed back against the wall, as he was pinned and could not move. His head was in a profile position, being turned and held in place. Suddenly, a larger black puff of smoke slammed him into his stomach, buckling him at his knees. He heard an angry, sadistic laughter, bellowing all around him. Curt felt that his life must have been bad. That he didn't do enough, because at this moment he must be in hell.

"Was it the church thing as a kid" he thought. "I was always good with my kids and raised them right. Granted I was outspoken… " His mind redirected to the pain he felt on his arms and legs as if someone was trying to snap his limbs. "Fuuuuccccckkk" he screamed out. "I'M BETTER THAN THIS!"

With all his might, he freed his left arm and grabbed one of the smoke puffs, which he realized were demons and squeezed it until it disappeared in his hand. Curt screamed out like a mad man, thrashing his body, until he was released from the hold of these demons. Curt spun and kicked and punched until the demons seem to disappear. One was still attached to his right ankle as Curt released a primal scream, smashing his left foot down upon it, watching it evaporate away.

Curt's heart rate was racing. His chest pounding as he tried to gather his thoughts and make sense of what just happened. He looked up and seen some angry looking jester like creatures coming at him. Their teeth were yellow, their eyes were bloodshot and their hair was all matted, under their clown hats. With their large feet and large hands, they came at Curt. The foul smell of body odor that smelled like death, permeated through Curt's nostrils, causing his eyes to swell up, temporarily blinding him by his own tears. Curt punched his left arm out as he flailed his right arm, hitting the clown in the middle and forcing the clown to his right to be knocked off balance. The punch he threw with his left hand hit squarely on the nose of the center clown. The clown's nose made a squeaky nose, like the balloon clown toy that he used to punch as a kid. The toy had sand in the bottom of the bag, forcing it back up at you. As the toy was hit, it would release a squeak and the motion would go on until you were done hitting it. The clown rocked back and rolled toward Curt like his old toy. Curt hit it again this time smashing the head off, causing an explosion which tossed curt into the air and smashing him down on the ground. He felt the painful kicks coming from both sides of his body, as the other two clowns were kicking him with feet that felt like the corner of a two x four smashing against his lower back and his chest and ribs.

Curt's first reaction was to place his body in a ball position, trying to protect him from the kicks. Curt mustered enough strength to kick his legs out, pushing himself away from the kicks as he was able to get up and run. The clowns smiled at Curt as they pulled out of nowhere running chainsaws. They came at Curt slowly as to taunt him with his soon to be demise. Curt was now backed against the furnace, where the demons grabbed him, holding his upper body firmly against the furnace. Curt screamed as the two chainsaws were being aimed at each of his shoulders. With a last ditch effort, Curt kicked his legs up hoping to hit the oversized hands holding the chainsaws, causing the chainsaws to hit together. Curt missed as the chainsaws were just about to slice him when the chains snapped and recoiled backwards hitting the clowns. As Curt fell to the ground hitting ass first on the concrete, the two remaining clowns fell backwards. Curt braced himself for an explosion again, but looked up and found himself in a cloud of white.

When the white cleared a hand extended down to Curt. Curt looked up and seen his best friend Mike. "I thought you needed my help." Mike had a wide smile on his face as he helped his friend off the ground. Curt was shocked to see Mike. But before he could say a word to his longtime friend a clown reappeared thrusting his chainsaw through Mike's back pushing it through his chest.

Curt screamed this time reacting to the clown and knocking him to the ground. He thrust his fists mightily into the head of the clown, knocking the yellow teeth out of its mouth. Curt grabbed a large brick and smashed it over the head of the clown, until it burst, throwing Curt across the room. Curt was dazed as he got up and seen that the clown as was his friend were gone.

Curt looked around and seen a ventriloquist doll sitting in front of another door. Curt was always freaked by these dolls. He knew now that they must be Satan's puppets. As he approached the doll, the doll began to laugh, lifting its wooden neck up and down. "So you got lucky, huh? Whadda ya expect from a punch of clowns," with an evil laugh, "you still need to get by me."

Curt had just experienced hell. He was battered and bruised and just seen his best friend, die in front of him again. He was in no way shape or form about to take any shit from a doll that freaked him out his whole life. He approached the doll, and as he grabbed its neck, ripping it off its body, "I'm not in the mood." Curt tossed the head and threw the body on the ground as he proceeded to go through the next door. Curt had succumbed to the fact that he was in Hell and he proceeded to put up with his penance. Not knowing what to expect, but wasn't in the mood to care, he banged the door open, being suddenly surprised.

Chapter 7 Heaven's Gate

Everything was white. Just like in all the old cliché movies about Heaven, Heaven was actually all white. Curt looked around, walking and turning to see if anything would appear. He looked down not able to see his feet through the perfectly white fog. He banged his foot to see what kind of surface he was walking on. The grounds seem to sink like a trampoline without the recoil. Curt decided to walk straight, expecting something or someone to appear. He walked and walked, but nothing appeared. His track of time began to become distorted.   He had been walking awhile, but was it 15 minutes, ½ hour, or even an hour. He was becoming confused. "Am I walking straight?" as he looked down with every step. "How long have I been walking?" He closed his eyes to try to retrieve his sense of direction.

Curt opened his eyes, to the sight of everything still white. Curt began to run, screaming "This can't be heaven... It's driving me crazy." Holding his head and again shutting his eyes, attempting to maintain his bearings.

He opened his eyes, as he felt he was about to run into something. He slowly opened them to more and more white. He tripped and fell over, losing his balance, as he had nothing to visualize his horizon against. His sense of balance was off and he felt nauseous. Curt lay on the ground, holding his hands over his eyes, keeping his eyes shut. It seemed like an instant, but could have been an eternity, that Curt laid on the ground. He tried to think of other things, such as how the ground felt. The ground felt soft underneath him, but was hard as a rock when he pulled his right hand down in a fist, to punch it. The ground wasn't hot, but wasn't cold either. He rolled over, laying belly flat on the ground, but yet he felt no temperature change. He opened his eyes, as he placed his nose on the ground, hoping to at least visualize the ground. But as he opened his eyes, he wasn't able to tell if he was looking up or down. All he seen on the ground was nothingness. He rolled onto his back, placing his forearm on his forehead, helping him to keep his eyes closed.

"I need to rest. I gotta figure out what's happening to me. I know I'm dead, but why do I still have all of my physical attributes? Why, can I still think? I gotta figure out what's going on. How long have I been at this? I can't tell how long has passed. I need a plan. I just gotta rest." Curt talking out loud, enjoying the fact that he could hear his own voice.

Curt tried to sleep, but lay there silent. He thought about his kids and if they were okay. " I wonder who found me dead?" he thought, hoping it wasn't his kids.

Curt thought about how long he had been in the white room. Could it already be days or weeks or even months?

He needed a plan to figure out how long a moment would last. "I need to figure out a concept of time" he thought "for my sanity, if for nothing else."

Curt got up and began counting to himself "one one thousand, two one thousand, three one thousand…" but this became too tedious and Curt would forget or stumble over his thoughts, confusing himself in the process.

Curt remembered during his biology class, his teacher telling him they needed to wash their hands for at least 30 seconds. His teacher equated that to two versus of the Happy birthday song. Curt began counting the letters of the alphabet on his hands. He counted four times to make sure his count was good as he counted up to the letter T, which was the twentieth letter of the alphabet. "So if I sing Happy Birthday to a name beginning with each letter up to the letter T, this would mean approximately 10 minutes have gone by. So what I will do is sing Happy Birthday up to the letter T and start over again, with the letter A, and I'll do this six times. To make sure I don't lose count, I'll keep count holding one finger out, until I have five outstretched fingers. I'll make a fist on number 6. Once I complete the 6th time, I'll stop and rest. At least I'll know how long I've been walking. I won't know how long I'll be resting, but I'll assume one hour on, and one hour off. It may not be right, but it will give me a sense of time. Even if it's my made up, in my own time." Evoking a smile on his face as he felt he had gained some control back. "I'll need to keep walking in one direction. I must make sure to lie down straight in the direction I was walking. I will take my shoes off; point them in the direction I was walking, placing one on each side of my body, so not too wake up from a rest confused, and head off back in the direction I came."

Curt didn't care if his plan was any good or not. All he was looking to do is head in one direction, and have some semblance of time. So that's what he did, singing happy birthday to Anna, Bill, Carol, Don, Edward, Frank, Ginny, Hanna, until he sang to Tom. He did this over and over and over, until he added up that he had been traveling for over 70 hours, mostly with his eyes closed. He figured he walked a fifteen minute mile, so that would be four miles per hour. Actually, he thought, two miles, because he would rest for one hour, more or less, he wasn't really sure, but would equal two miles every hour of time. So all he had to remember was how many hours went by, double it to get how far he had walked.

Curt had just finished his 72th hour, realizing again, how strange it was not to be thirsty or hungry. He stood up thinking maybe he would do a double shift on the ground to rest, but knew this would really start to distort his sense of time. Curt figured at the 100th hour he would come up with a new game plan. Curt stood up, opening his eyes, placed his hands in front of him to give him a sense of horizon, when he noticed through his fingertips a dot.

"Are my eyes going blurry" he thought as he closed and reopened to see if he could still see the dot.

The dot was still there. With everything white he couldn't tell how close he was to the dot or even what it could be. He knew he would have to travel toward the dot. Curt felt invigorated, because even if the dot turned out to be nothing, he now had a goal to find out what it was and finally had a direction to aim at. The dot didn't grow quickly. Another 24 hours had passed, before he noticed the color of the dot was golden. Another 48 hours passed, before he knew for sure what he was seeing. Once he had seen the color, he figured it had to be the Gates to Heaven. Finally, after 6 days of walking, he could finally make out the gates. Curt knew that it would now just take him 24 more hours to reach the gates. It took God 7 days to create the heavens and earth, so this trek must be 7 days long to acknowledge his feat.

Curt reached the gates expecting to see St. Peter, but no one was there. Every story he had heard always had St. Peter telling them that they may enter or turn them away. "Maybe it's not my time, maybe I'm supposed to head back" as Curt turned looking at nothing but white again. "You gotta be shittin' me if they think I'm doing that walk again" Curt announced as if he had an audience listening.

"Curt. My God, it's you. Oh, how I've missed you." A voice was heard over Curt's shoulder. The voice was soft and reassuring. It didn't take him long to figure whose voice it was.

"Mom?" He said softly, as if he was unsure that he even heard anything. Curt turned and looked back at the large Pearly gates. He didn't see anyone and he yelled out "MOM?" as he began to run alongside the gates, until he seen a figure on the other side, staring at him, like only a proud mom could look at a child.

"Oh, how I've prayed that I would see you again. Oh, how I've missed you." Tears rolled down his mother's face. "My boy, my boy, come here."

"Mom, mom, mom" Curt repeated himself as not to believe his eyes. "Mom, I've missed you too. There wasn't a day gone by I didn't think of you." He reached for his mother's hands through the rungs of the gate. "I knew you'd be in heaven, I knew it." As Curt attempted to touch his mother's hands an electrical shock threw him on to the ground.

"Honey, don't…" His mother June tried to warn him but was too late. "I'm sorry honey. You can't touch me, they don't allow it." His mom stated, with an embarrassment and concern on not warning Curt quicker. However, after 15 years of not seeing her son, she was only thinking of seeing him. "Everything is different now honey, everything. This isn't the same place anymore." June told

Curt that Heaven was no longer the Heaven he was taught growing up.

Chapter 8 Where's Dad?

Looking confused and anxious, Curt began to pace back in forth. As he reached towards the fence to grab his mother's hand the ground opened up between them, placing an infinitely deep moat of nothing between them. "What's going on?" Curt questioned "Heaven's not heaven, I reach for you and the ground opens up? Mom, is it really you?"

"It's okay." June stated in her eternal maternal voice. "I need you to listen to me, it's important and I don't have a lot of time. There are guards here and if they catch me..." June stopped in mid sentence and immediately changed direction in what she was saying. "You have to find your dad; he'll fill you in the details."

"Where is dad? He's not in heaven?"

"Oh, honey. Did you really think you find your father in heaven?" June said half heartedly, trying to diminish fears in Curtis.

"He didn't make it?" Paleness poured into Curt's face, from the blood draining from his head, making his skin as white as the world around him.

A smile on June's face quickly reassured Curtis. "He's fine. Well he was fine. I mean he was here, but left to find your Grandfather. Your grandpa is a hero up here. Tough old guy, well, actually he's not that old up here. He's on a mission. Your grandfather has a lot of integrity. Out of all the souls up here, he was considered the most trustworthy. However, when he hadn't come back, your father set out to find him. Your father always looked out for his dad and now I need you to look out for your dad. It's your destiny."

"My destiny? Me? I'm nothing. My whole life has been a waste, mom. After you died, then dad, I have done nothing but struggle. I've been a good dad, with my kids. I've got great kids, mom. I love them more than anything. But the rest of my life has been in shambles."

"There is a reason for everything. I have seen your children. I was allowed to see you with them. They still need you. Your time isn't ready. You need to change what is happening here or everyone, everywhere will suffer for eternity."

Suddenly, others came up to Curt's mom and begged her to leave now. "They are coming, please they will hurt you. Let your mother leave if you love her."

Calmly, June told Curtis "Find you father and grandfather. Your heart will lead you to them as it has brought you to me."

As the others tugged frantically at June and begging for Curtis to let her leave. Curt in a panic yelled "Go. Go NOW. I swear to God I'll find dad. GO. GO. GOOOO!"

Reluctantly, June looked back at her son, her eyes filled with tears. Did she send him on a suicide mission? She knew it was the only hope the remaining souls in Heaven had. She believed her son could conquer all and this was his moment. As June disappeared in a cloud of white, the gates of Heaven suddenly pulled closer to Curt, as the moat had suddenly disappeared. He ran to the gate and reached in as if to be able to somehow grab his mother and bring her to safety. As he reached in, he suddenly seen a scaly looking human, like something he had seen as a kid watching Voyage to the Bottom of the Sea.   Curtis stepped back as the large eyed creature approached. The fingers on this monster looked like they were three times the size of Curt's fingers. The arms that looked scaly, looked more tattooed than scales as the creature moved within five feet of Curt. The arms were muscular as were the legs, especially the size of the thighs. As the creature approached the fence, the oversized eyes, which seem to take up half the creature's face turned from extremely black to a blood filled red. The nose was missing and there were no ears on the creature, except for two holes where the nose should be and a large hole on each side of his head which seemed to be dripping pus and blood. The teeth were like claws as the creature grabbed the golden bars and screamed like a trapped animal trying to escape.

Curt was afraid for his mom as he heard her let out a blood curdling scream. He stared at the creature with large black heads and warts covering the face. "Come get me asshole", as Curt tried to buy time for his mother's escape.

With a high pitched roar the creature snapped the bars in its hand and then struggled to fit through the opening it caused. Curt stepped back, knowing it was time to run. Curt took two steps back, one with his right foot and one with his left, before turning to run. As he glanced at the creature as he turned, Curt lost his footing and fell, extending his hands out to break his fall, knowing he would have to get away quick as the creature would be just about upon him. Curt extended his arms, but suddenly realized he was falling farther and farther down as he was freefalling into white space. Curt looked down and spotted he was falling toward ground as trees and water suddenly came into view. "Holeeeeeey Shit!" Curt realized he would shortly come in contact with the ground.

He braced himself, covering his face with his arms and curling up in a fetal position expecting the impact of the ground. He hit the ground hard. The ground had very little forgiveness as Curt landed on his side, before rolling backwards as his body came in contact with the side of a dead apple tree. Curt felt a moment of pain, but instantly the pain dissipated. He stood up in disbelief, as he wiped his shoulders and arms. He Bent over and feeling his knees, before he slowly straightened back up. "That fall should have killed me!" He thought to himself, before realizing again, that he was already dead.

Chapter 9 The Cries For Help

Curt became aware that wherever he fell, the creature didn't follow. As he peered into the sky, making sure no creature was falling toward him; all he noticed were white clouds and blue sky. Along the ground of tall grass lay red delicious apples that were so tempting to eat. As Curt picked one up and stared at it, he noticed the apple did not have one flaw on it. He looked and noticed that the only apple tree was dead. Yet these apples on the ground weren't rotting. "God must have one good refrigeration unit to keep these apples fresh." Knowing that the apples must have been there a long time, based on the fact the tree was dead.

"Really? Do you think it's a bloody good idea to eat that apple?" A beautiful blonde woman in a checkered dress asked. "Isn't that how we got in this mess to begin with?"

Curt turned, shocked by the sound of another human voice, yet was also embarrassed by the fact that he had actually thought about biting into the apple. The apple dropped out of his hand to the ground, his hands shown palm up to this beautiful stranger, in a move that replicated a small child showing his hands after getting caught in the cookie jar. "I wasn't gonna eat that." As the words spoken made him look and sound guiltier than he was.

"Too bad, they are really delicious." As the woman bent over and picked one up, taking a bite out of it. "Red Delicious, my favorite."

"I thought you couldn't eat that?" He Questioned. "What about the whole Adam and Eve thing?"

"...and you thought that this tree" the woman begins laughing, interrupting her own thought "don't worry; this isn't the Tree of Knowledge of Good and Evil. There was a whole garden you know that they could eat from. I mean it is the Garden of Eden."

"I know" embarrassed by the fact he didn't know. Curt looked up at the woman for the first time and realized who he had been talking to. "Oh my God, your princess Diana"

"I didn't think you recognized me" her British accent seeming even more noticeable. "I hope you understand that I am not a princess here, but just another soul trying to help. Are you here to help? There are so many imposters, it sometimes tough to know."

"Help? I don't know why I'm here, or, what's going on. I just seen my mother behind the pearly gates and she sent me to look for my father and grandfather. She said it's my destiny. I mean, how can it be my destiny? All I did was trip and bang my head and now I'm here. Is this Heaven?"

"I don't know? Did you watch Field of Dreams? That turned out to be Iowa." As a smile and twinkle came from Lady Diana's eye. "What's your name?"

"Curt."

"Your June and Bill's son. You do resemble your father." Diana examined his facial features.

"How do you know my parents?" Curt completely shocked regarding Diana's knowledge of who his parents are. "What's going on here?"

"God has a plan. We are all part of God's plan. You will soon find out what plan has been laid out for you. We are all in this together. We mustn't fail or we will all be lost souls forever. Your mum is a beautiful person inside and out. I have had the honor of spending much time with her. She truly is a Saint."

"Yeah, she put up with my father and ungrateful kids her whole life." Curt sarcastically placed his two cents into the conversation.

"Don't sell yourself, your father, or anyone else short. We need you. Your mother has all the confidence in the world in you." Diana paused. "I need you to listen very carefully." Diana's smile faded from her face as she became more direct with Curt. "You were not exactly our first choice. However, your grandfather and father are very strong souls. Your mum is confident you're the man to help us. You will need many souls to help you along your way. Your mum and everyone else behind the Pearly Gates are in trouble. This is why your father and grandfather are not there. They are battling a war."

"...a war? What is going on?"

"Please do not interrupt. You must show restraint. I will explain what I can now, before I send you on your way." Diana perturbed by Curt's interruption.

"On my way? Where?" Curt blurting out his unfortunate thirst for knowledge, as Diana just glared at him. Curt mumbled "Sorry" as he looked at Diana, before dropping his eyes.

After a moment of silence, Diane continued. "We have a long way to go. Please follow me and no matter what, please don't interrupt until I complete what I need to tell you. You will have plenty of time for questions", Diana bent down and picked up and apple and handed it to Curt. "Eat this, maybe it will help keep you quiet!" Diana softened her tone "I especially hope you have the dignity of not talking with food in your mouth." As Diana placed her hand on Curt's hand and gently pulled him in the direction she began walking. As she lightly released her hand from his, Diana began to speak to Curt again. This time she wasn't interrupted.

"Your father is a bit of a character. He isn't one for taking direction very well. Your grandfather needs to constrain your father. He has quite the temper. Your father seen what was happening and was the first to lead a group of souls. They are heading to Hades. Your grandfather has gone after him with his earthly best friend Joe. They are two very strong men. They grew up together in Germany; they escaped Nazi persecution by coming to America. They never once had an argument. They respect each other tremendously. They are kings among kings. Joe died of a broken heart weeks after your grandfather passed on. They helped each other in good times and in bad times. They are extremely honorable men. You were blessed with an incredible grandfather. You already knew this. We need to know if you have the same integrity and honor as your dad's dad. We must expose any weakness you possess and see if you can learn from this weakness. You have passed a few tests already with the clowns and letting your mother go, to save her. These test are nothing compared to what you will see, going forward. Your heart filled with anger, knowing your mother is in jeopardy. We need to know if you can adjust to the pain of your heart being filled with sorrow and carrying on. This journey will not be easy. We need to know if you're capable of succeeding. Now you can ask questions."

As they walked through the Garden of Eden the trees colors were vibrant as if in the peak of Autumn. As they carried on walking through the deciduous forest, Curt kept his focus on Diana's words. "You keep saying we. Who are you talking about?"

"All of the good souls. The corruption of earth has decreased our strength. This will need to change or we will be lost forever."

Curt's voice deepened as he inquired into his next question, "You mentioned war. This is a war of good and evil isn't it?"

"Yes and we are losing."

"What about God? Why doesn't he help if he exists?" Curt stopped walking as he glared directly into Diana's eyes, not feeling intimidated for the first time in her presence.

"Oh, he exists. His energy is the purest energy to touch you. God is pure. However, God's energy is weakening. The loss of belief in him has weakened his energy. God has been taken, we believe, to the depths of Hell. Your father is on a mission to find God. You are on a mission to find God. We all need to find God. God is father to us all. If you are successful you will feel the presence of the Almighty."

Before Curt could ask another question, he began to hear an inaudible sound or screech that was becoming louder and louder. "We are coming close; I need to leave you now. Your journey starts here. I wish you the best. Now head in this direction", Diana pointing straight ahead, in the direction of the inaudible noise "and you will find out if you will be able to handle your journey."

Curt looked straight ahead before turning to Diana, "Where will you be," but his question was never answered as Diana vanished at the edge of the Garden of Eden.

Curt continued on what he found to be his quest. He thought of what Diana said and how he needed to succeed. Curt thought to himself the obvious questions "Why me? I'm not successful in life. I couldn't keep a marriage together. I have friends, but wouldn't even consider myself close to being popular. Why me? I must be part of line that can't be broken. My grandfather was a great man, my father was far from perfect, but always had a good heart. My kids are awesome. I hope they're okay. I already miss them. I must be in a line of greatness in my family. I'm guessing I just need not break the chain". Curt felt humbled as he continued to walk toward the sound that was becoming louder. "It's not me they need at all. They need my family. I need my family."

The sounds that Curt walk towards became louder and louder. "What is that sound?" He listened to the noise trying to decipher what he was hearing. "Oh..."as he paused, before completing his thought "...my God", as it occurred to him what he was hearing. He walked closer and closer, understanding with certainty what he was hearing.

The sound was now very clear and very loud. "Why are so many crying? Why are they crying in pain?"

Curt walked up to a doorway of a building looked to be made of stainless steel. As he grabbed the handle to enter, the coldness of the handle sent an ice pain down his spine. He knew he needed to enter. He knew something was clearly wrong and he needed to help. As he fought the pain traveling thru his body, he felt an even stronger pain as he opened the door and stepped inside. The cold pain he felt was something he forgot about from his own childhood. Curt had been sliding on the lake, behind his aunt and uncle's home, with his sisters and cousins. Curt was sliding on the ice with his rubberized snow boots. His mother had placed Wonder bread plastic bags in his boots to help keep his feet warmer and dry. However, no amount of plastic bags would help him on this day. As this 6 year old boy stepped backwards to get a good running start, so he could get a super long slide, he stepped back where the ice wasn't frozen. As his left leg reached back for his final step, before going forward, a moment of warmth traveled thru his body as he seemed to be suspended over the open water. His yarn knitted gloves weren't a match as he attempted to grab the ice as he went in feet first, falling backwards into the depths of lake. Curt's green hooded jacket, puffed to help keep him warm, never had a chance once his body submerged into the frigid landscape. The instantaneous pain throughout his body from the cold was unbearable. Curt had not only fallen into the water, but had slid beneath the ice.

A week earlier, Curt had watched a movie about Houdini with his father. Curt remembered the one scene where Houdini fell through the ice. He remembered Houdini gasping for air in ice pockets as he tried to find his way out. Houdini did it, Curt thought, so can he. Curt noticed a black spot under the ice and placed his mouth on it, just like the movie. It was an air pocket. Curt got the deepest breadth he was able to and listened to the sound of running water. He knew he had to go toward the running water. He pushed off the ice and headed toward the sound of running water, kicking his feet and flailing his hands the best he possibly could. The cold he had felt seemed to have gone, as a calm thinking 6 year old, kept his wits and lunged toward the sound of the mini waterfall. In some ways, this was the most mature moment in Curt's life. Even at this young age, he knew what he had to do to survive. Death never even seemed like a possibility.

As his breath was leaving his body, Curt's right arm felt the solid corner of the ice, where the water ran freely. He pulled himself back to the spot where he fell in. He came up for air, as he tried to pull himself out of the frigid water, but was too exhausted. He tried to cry for help, but had no energy to make a sound. He somehow managed to get both hands on top of the ice, where his gloves seemed to freeze, latching him like safety gear. As he made another attempt to get himself out to no avail, his sister spotted him and screamed for him to hang on as she pulled him up from the possible depths of Hell. As she helped him walk back to the house, the pain of every nerve in his body seemed to explode. His body shivered uncontrollably. As he entered the house, a panicked father and mother seen him as they had just received word of the accident from Curt's little cousin, just moments before. A relieved, yet teary eyed parents quickly undressed him out of his wet clothes. His aunt ran a luke warm bath as they slowly tried to raise his core temperature back up. After what seem to be hours in a bathtub, Curt's mom placed warm pajamas, a robe, and a blanket around him, then held him close as he shivered. The coldness would not leave his body for three days. As Curt snuggled with his mom, he remembered what seemed like a push back toward the open water. Looking back, Curt was flailing his arms and legs, but they went in all directions. He knew where he had to go, but he couldn't and knew he didn't do it on his own. Somebody else helped him. Curt never mentioned to this to anyone.

The feeling of this pain had escaped him for 36 years, until now. The cold dissipated as he walked into a large room made of marble. He looked ahead and seen an old woman holding a cloth in her hand. "Excuse me," Curt yelled to the woman. "Excuse me, can I help? What can I do? Why are they crying in pain?"

The old woman looked up at Curt. A cold stare of disapproval of Curt was written all over her. "You want to help? You should have thought of that, years ago." The old woman snapped at Curt. "Have your fun and don't worry about the consequences. People like you have no remorse for life. I questioned the existence of God in my final years on earth. I questioned why if there was a God, so much pain and suffering that occurred. Disease, starvation, killings, I thought I seen it all. Now I'm here, dealing with mutilations."

"Mutilations? My God they're just babies. The screams I heard are all babies. How? Why? Who?"

"You, and many others", the understandably bitter old woman exclaimed. "You take your life for granted, but not that of the children."

Curt looked at the woman and recognized who she was. It was Mother Theresa. She was angry, very angry. She had a right to be angry. She was dealing with 1000's of mutilated children, all crying for help. Curt looked up and seen and endless amount of bassinettes, all filled with crying babies. "Where did they come from?"

"Come here get a closer look." Mother Theresa demanded of Curt.

Curt walked up to the bassinette where Mother Theresa was standing and looked down at the infant. He turned his head away from what he saw. "What happened?"

"Every one of these children are all lost souls, waiting for the day to be claimed or seek vengeance. They were all throwaways from earth. They were discarded like they didn't matter. Look at this child!" Mother Theresa reached up grabbing Curt by the chin and forcibly making him look. "A few minutes of fun, suddenly the woman is pregnant, gets an abortion, and the child ends up here. Their limbs are shredded off their bodies. They are treated like waste and dumped like waste. Look at this poor little boy, his arm ripped from his body, his leg shredded from the doctor's scalpel. They are a mess. How can I help them all? There are too many. I can only wait until they are claimed."

"Oh God, no..." He dropped to his knees at the feet of Mother Theresa. Curt grabbed the bottom of her habit, gripping his hands as if the fabric had become part of his fist. His head fell forward above his clenched hands as he begged for forgiveness. "Please forgive me", tears rolling out of his tightly shut eyes, "my child is here. I pleaded with her not to have one. I tried to stop her but I couldn't".

Curt's body shook hysterically as he loosened his grip forcing his hands and head to fall hard against the marble floor, with his hands taking the majority of the blow. Mother Theresa stood over him, her shoulder already rolled forward from years of hard labor helping out the sick and poor. She placed her hand gently on Curt's back as if she had just place her hand on the Bible. "Get up.

Get a hold of yourself." She softly spoke. "I will help you. I can help you. Please, get up."

Curt pushed off his hands and sat on his knees, looking up at Mother Theresa. His eyes had already swollen and bloodshot from the tears. He took a deep breath as he tried to compose himself. His eyes had seen the strength in this old woman's eyes. Curt dropped his head again in shame, took another deep breath and mustered up all the strength he had to stand back up. "My girl friend had one." His voice cracked in disgrace. "I went to the clinic that day. She didn't know I would show. She went there with a girlfriend. She had already made up her mind. She said we were too young."

"What happened?"

"I begged for her not to go through with it. I told her I loved her and we could make it work. I told her I would love this child more than life itself. Anna smiled at me. That was her name. She said she had to and that was best for us. She asked me to leave and she would call me when she got home. Anna said everything would be okay. I left the clinic, despondent. I swear there isn't a day gone by I haven't thought of my unborn child. I am so sorry that I wasn't strong enough or man enough ..." Curt sighed as he looked back into the eyes of an understanding Mother Theresa. Curt changed his thought pattern and just said "...I'm sorry." Curt wiped the tears on the sleeve of his t-shirt.

Curt stared as he anticipated his punishment for his part in denying life to this child. He didn't care, he knew it was time for his punishment and did not care how severe it was, because, he deserved it. "Let me show you something. Follow me; you aren't going to like what you see." Her voice stern, she turned and began to walk. "I want you to look and learn."

Curt followed in tow as they walked between the pink and blue bassinettes . As they passed by each child, Mother Theresa softly whispered a hush that seemed to comfort each child they walked by. Curt felt nauseas, as he stared at each infant he walked passed. Arms missing, legs missing, spines twisted, heads and chests punctured, necks snapped. Children were white, black, brown, yellow, and red, who had all suffered the mutilation of being aborted. As they turned past the babies toward another room, Curt looked back at the last pink bassinet. A beautiful black little girl with her head looking up as her twisted body had her chest against the mattress and her shoulder blades to the sky caught Curt's eye. Her right arm moved in excitement awkwardly as she attempted to move it freely from the restraints of her twisted torso. Her left arm was gone from her shoulder. Her legs bent at the knee as she kicked her legs, exposing her right leg missing an ankle and foot. Mother Theresa turned back at Curt noticing him staring at this child and responded "Such a happy little one, always smiling, and such a shame."

Chapter 10 The Consequence Of Ignorance

"Many children like that one, so happy, yet so alone," as Mother Theresa entered into the next room. "Come, follow me. I want to show you something." As the two walked into the dark room with sunlight coming in halfway through, splitting the room, Mother Theresa stopped and turned toward Curt. "Do you believe in the Bible?"

"I guess. I'm no expert. I don't know individual passages." Curt remarked as he kept turning around toward the children in the other room.

"I'm sure you heard of an eye for an eye?"

"Yeah, why?" still distracted in his thoughts of the babies.

"In this room, aborted children meet their parents. There will be a woman entering through the door on the other side. Let me tell you about her. She grew up spoiled. Came from an affluent family who thought they were infallible. She came home pregnant the first time at age 17. Her mother and father both advised her that she was too young for a child. The shame and embarrassment her pregnancy would bring couldn't and wouldn't be allowed.

She was told to have an abortion. Her father coldly told her to get it taken care of right away. Her mother went with her to have it done. So she had the abortion. Her parents told her to forget about it because the baby would have ruined her life. About 2 years later, she became pregnant again. This time she was away at college. She became drunk at a party. Drunk enough to be amorous but sober enough to know what she was doing. She went back to her dorm with a man she just met. Used protection, but nothing is 100 percent. When she confided in him that she was with child, he sounded just like her father. At least she told him, the first time she was pregnant, the boy never knew. Anyhow, he told her the same thing, that a baby would ruin their lives. He went with her to get the abortion. I guess he wanted to make sure that it was done, because she never heard from him again after the procedure was complete. Procedure...," shaking her head," even I have started trivializing these poor, poor children. May God forgive my callousness? "

Curt placed his hand on the nun's shoulder. "I know you care, very much for these children. Don't be so hard on yourself. You were a great woman in life and in death or whatever this place is."

"Purgatory. We are in Purgatory. Decisions are made into which direction we will go. I am here to help. I questioned God's existence in the final years of my life. That is probably why I'm here. I lost faith being around so much despair. But I must tell you quickly about this woman, because she will be here soon." Mother Theresa pointed at the door straight ahead in the bright light. "She finally settled down and was married to a very good man. She was excited to find out she was pregnant. Now a child wouldn't be a burden to her lifestyle. Tragically, her husband was killed in an auto accident. A month later she had her third abortion. She had a late term abortion. Told her friends and family she lost the baby. She made a tragic figure of herself. She was taught not to love these children. She never once gave their lives a second thought. She eventually remarried, had no kids, and lived a selfish self absorbed life. She died of cancer and is now about to meet her fate. Now your job is to tell her this."

Curt looked shocked. "Tell her what? Tell her what her fate is. Tell her she is going to hell? No, no, no, you got the wrong guy."

"You're the right guy. You're going to tell her. On earth, I could tell a man that someday he would give up his worldly possessions and come help me with the poor. Guess what, they always came, without question. You will do this without question, because it is your fate."

"What do I say" Curt asked honestly confused.

"You will figure it out. I must go as I have work to do. The children need me." Mother Theresa walked back toward the entrance, leading back to the infants.

As Curt tried to follow, she shooed him back stepping toward him and lifting her fragile arms up and motioning her wrists up toward Curt. As fragile a woman she was, Curt stood motionless as she turned around and left the room, the door shutting behind her.   Curt walked toward the door, but it had disappeared into a solid wall. Suddenly, the sound of another door opening was heard across the room. Curt turned his head to see a dark haired woman standing in the rays of the sun. "I must be in heaven" she stated.

"It's Purgatory." Curt advised the woman, who looked stunned hearing another voice. "I guess I'm here to help you."

"Purgatory?" the woman questioned. "I have led a wonderful life. I have always taken care of myself. I have never burdened anyone. I have always been self sufficient. I admit, I'm not perfect, but who is?"

"The almighty is."Curt responded with the only answer that came to his head. "We all needed to live a life without sin. Purgatory is where we come to find out our fate."

"…and you will tell me my fate? Will I be with my first husband? I truly loved him."

"I don't know. I'm not sure why I am doing this. Mother Theresa stated that I need to talk to you about, I don't know, your life, I guess." As he sounded less and less confident in what he was to do.

"Mother Theresa? THE Mother Theresa? You're telling me, that Mother Theresa sent you to talk to me. Please, I realize I'm dead, but Mother Theresa? " The woman kept repeating her name and giving it less credibility each time she said it. Who are you to tell me my fate?"

"I'm no one. I'm just a guy who smacked his head on concrete and now I'm here. I have a lot of questions myself I need answered. I am just trying to figure this all out. All I know is what I've been told..."

"...by Mother Theresa? I would like to meet her myself" The woman brushed her shoulder length hair with her hands, mocking Curt as if he had just lied to her. "Where is she? Let's go."

"If she wanted to meet with you she would have stayed. Can I ask you your name?"

"It's Kim. What's yours?"

"I'm Curt"

"Well, Curt, I don't mean to be curt, Curt, but why would she meet with you and not with me?"

"I guess we all have a destiny we need to fulfill. I guess our lives, I mean after lives might be predestined. I honestly don't know. All I do know is we are here together now, both trying to figure out our paths in this afterlife? Have you seen anyone else?" Curt, began to question Kim, in order to find out what is in store for both of them.

"No... have you?" Kim sharply responded.

Not wanting to mention his time with Lady Diana, because she wouldn't believe him anyway, Curt acknowledged "I've seen my mother; I'm looking for my father."

"I hope to see my father, and my first husband, that would be wonderful." A smile came across Kim's face as she spoke of the men most important in her life. "Do I just wish to see them?"

"I don't think it works that way. So I understand you never had kids?"

"How do you know that? Who are you?" Kim looking nervous as Curt finally released what Mother Theresa had told him.

"I'm nobody, really. Just what Moth..."

"Mother Theresa told you." Kim interrupted Curt in mid sentence.

Curt's short fuse became lit. "Listen lady, I'm just trying to figure this shit out. If you want me to help you, I'll try. But you have to understand, none of this is in mine or your control."

"Well, I'm not leaving anything about me, in your control. How do I get out of here?"

"Don't know, don't care. I guess we will be here as long as it takes." Curt, walked away toward the wall that no longer had the door, sat on the floor, leaning his back against the cold stainless steel wall. "I guess I've got all of eternity."

"...and I am not planning on spending it with you." Kim pointed out. She turned away heading directly opposite of where Curt sat down. Kim walked away, but every time she was just out of sight, she ended up unintentionally walking back toward Curt. After numerous attempts to get away, she reluctantly walked back a final time toward him, screamed at the top of her lungs, before composing herself, settling next to Curt on the floor. Kim crossed her hands in front of her knees. With her head down in her lap, she sighed. "What do I have to do to get away from you?" Kim looked up as she turned her head toward Curt.

Kim's hair covered her face as if she was using it to form a wall between her and Curt. Curt looked at her knowing where the conversation was headed, turned away, looking straight ahead and asked "Why didn't you have kids."

"By the time I met my second husband, neither of us wanted kids. We were in our mid thirties and were already set in our ways."

"What about kids with your first husband?" Curt questioned already knowing the answer.

"I miscarried after he was killed." Kim responded, believing her own lies from years of stating her, self pity story on others. Silence came upon both of them, as Curt didn't know how to respond. They both just sat there for a few minutes before Kim looked at Curt "WHAT?"

"We both know that's not true."

"Yes, IT IS" Kim sharply snapped back.

"You have had three abortions. The third one was a late term abortion."

"How do you kno..." Kim hitting Curt with both hands as she began to cry "Why are you doing this to me?"

Curt deflected her hands as he moved out of harm's way. "You have to be honest. You have to be honest with yourself." Curt watched Kim place her hands between her knees bawling her eyes out. "I had a girlfriend, who had an abortion. I couldn't stop her from having it. I guess that's why we are here. It must be our penance. "

"So I had abortions, so what. I was too young the first time, too stupid the second, and too distraught the third time. I guess I never really wanted children, but Dan, my husband, I mean, my first husband, wanted kids. So when he died, I didn't want to raise a child alone."

"You were in your third trimester. Why didn't you give your child up for adoption? I knew a guy whose wife delivered a preemie at six months. They had a beautiful little girl." Curt knowingly overstepped his boundaries in questioning the late term abortion.

"Please, be real. I wasn't going to raise a child alone and clearly I wasn't about to give the child up for adoption. What would everyone think of me? So I told everyone I had a miscarriage. What difference does it make?"

"The difference is you killed a human life. Not one, but three. Now I don't pretend to know when life starts, but I do know they have a fighting chance in the third trimester." Curt lecturing Kim as she now placed her hands over her head, using her forearms to cover her ears.

"Shut up, just shut up. You didn't live my life, okay? You don't know my life, okay? I did what I thought was best for me. I have no regrets."

After a brief period of silence, Curt softly spoke "I regretted my childhood sweetheart's abortion every single day of my life. " Again he paused before continuing, "When I had children years later, I thought of what should have been my oldest child in the waiting room, waiting to see and hold her new brother and sister for the first time. "Curt's eyes began to tear up "I really blew it, I should have fought harder for her".

"Maybe, I'm here to tell you that you need to get over it. That it doesn't matter." Kim turned the tables to look as if they were in her favor.

Before Curt could respond a voice came from in front of them. "Kim?" A stern voice bellowed throughout.

"Dan? Oh my God, Dan!" Kim jumped to her feet running towards a figure now within sight. Kim threw her arms around him, squeezing him as her head lay upon his chest.

Dan was about six foot 2, with wavy blonde hair. He looked to be in great shape. He looked to be about 220 pounds of solid muscle. His pects could be seen through his tightly fitting blue, short sleeve t=shirt. He grabbed Kim's arms and pulled her away. Her five six slim frame was poised to look up at Dan. She smiled looking into his eyes, but he didn't. After a moment, the smile went away from Kim's face. "What's wrong? Aren't you glad to see me?"

Dan's hands moved down toward Kim's. His hands folding over hers like a pair of gloves. "I would like you to meet someone. Danny, it's time."

A small boy with blonde hair like his dad walked up putting his arms around his father's left leg, barely being able to clasp them together. Danny was no more than three years old. A solemn look was on the boy's face as he looked at his dad and then over to Kim.

"This is my child. He is a beautiful little boy, isn't he? He came to me only a month after I came here."

"That's our child? My God, he's beautiful. Hi Danny. " Kim leaned down, bending at the knees to be at the child's eye level. "Am I your mom? You're a sweetheart." Kim reached her hand toward the boy's face, in an effort to show him affection.

"Grrrrrrrrrrrr", as the small child's face changed from innocent to ferocious. His eyes bulged from their sockets, veins protruded from the sides of his head, and his small smile opened like a rabid dog. Danny lunged at Kim tearing a chunk of flesh out of her arm.

"NOOO, HELP ME" Kim screamed as she pulled back falling back on to the ground, kicking her feet as she tried to push herself away.

Dan grabbed the child, placing himself between Danny and Kim. "It's ok son, it's all over." Dan calmly spoke to his son. Danny looked into his dad's eyes and began to cry. Dan held him tight, as he picked him up, the child cuddled inside his dad's arm, looking for comfort. Dan turned back towards Kim, looking at the fear in her eyes, as she held her right arm over her bleeding left arm. "I'm sorry that happened. I thought you should meet the one person, who had given you the opportunity to do the right thing. I'm sorry how everything turned out. Let's go little buddy. Everything will be okay. You will always have me." Dan turned with his son in his arms and disappeared in the light.

"My arm, my arm;" Kim cried in pain. "Help me, please."
Kim turned toward Curtis who looked at her in fear.

Curt took a step toward Kim, but was shot back in the face,
by an invisible fist, knocking him on his ass. Curt, was
dazed, attempting to shake off an unexpected cold cock to
the face, that he hadn't felt since it happened to him in his
younger years, when a bar fight broke out. Curt had
turned and a young punk just punched him for no
apparent reason. If not for his buddy Nick jumping in and
grabbing the young punk, Curt may have found himself in
trouble, as the young punk was all set to start stomping on
Curt. Curt, backed away, covering his head in self defense.
However, he smashed the back of his head on the cold
steel wall behind him. Curt attempted to gather his senses
as he looked forward toward Kim. Kim had staggered to
her feet, still holding her arm, as she turned from side to
side, not knowing what to do or where to go. Kim looked
at Curt pleading to him, "What's going on?"

Before Curt could answer, the deafening cries of a child
came from Kim's left side. Suddenly a distinctly different
child's scream came from her right side. Kim looked left
and then right following the second scream. "Mom,
mommy help me mommy." A small child's voice was
heard.

Kim turned back left at the sound of the voice, but
suddenly shrieked when she felt something touch her right
arm. "Help me first, mommy." Kim screamed at the sight

of the child. The grey skin of an infant the size of a seven year old grabbed a hold of her wrist. "Help me first mommy, 'cause I was your first."

"No, mommy, no" Kim's left wrist was grabbed. "He's always first mommy, I'm your first little girl."

Kim's eyes were showed fear. Her mouth wide open, but not a sound came out. Her extreme fear was if she were in a nightmare, but wasn't able to wake up. Kim could not move, except for the shaking of her weakening legs. She would have collapsed but the two children seem to hold her up by stretching her in opposite directions. "NNNNOOOO" she finally screamed out as the two children simultaneously released her as she fell hard on to her knees.

In unison, the two children, bloodied and shredded, spoke to Kim. The girl was missing part of her arm at the elbow, while the boy's stomach was gashed wide open. "Why did you hurt us mommy, why?" Kim tried to hide but the two children grabbed her by her shoulders and whipped her back, slamming her back to the ground. Kim lied there helpless as the two children lay upon her. The two grew bigger into adult size, but their looks never changed from their fetal growth. The voices became angry as they tugged hard under the armpit of their mother. Their angry look, with a toothless scowl, tightly wrapped their arms around Kim's. Again together they spoke, "This is what it feels like to be abandoned and aborted." The two pulled

with the strength of a 100 as they tore the limbs from
Kim's body. First, were the arms, followed by the legs.

The boy walked around her, picking up her limbs, as the
girl shoved her amputated arm, into the side of Kim's jaw.
The girl grabbed with her bloody stump and her one good
arm and straightened Kim's head and told her "Watch".

Kim turned away, so the boy took her limbs and forced
them through her abdomen, screaming "WATCH!" Kim's
stumped body jerked her head upwards as she experience
pain beyond any threshold of measuring. She could only
gasp as her still open, glazed eyes were directly staring at
the two.   "That is for never giving us any of your
attention."

The girl followed with, "This is what you missed out on,
getting rid of us." Soon the oversized fetuses shrunk in
size to the size of healthy new born infants. They slowly
grew to a 6 month old, a 1 year old, 2, 4, 8, 10, 13, 16, 21,
until they both reached their adult age they would be at
the time of Kim's earthly death. "We would have grown to
be good people, instead we are nothing. We are worse
than nothing, we are garbage."

An image of a bloody plastic bag be thrown into a
dumpster went through Kim's mind. The image of the bag
getting crushed by other debris and other bloody bags
became very vivid in her mind. As if a movie camera
zoomed in on the bag, Kim realized that was her daughter

in the bag.   A tear rolled down Kim's eyes as she realized how selfish her life was. She looked to her two grown children with eyes seeking forgiveness. "Yeah, right." Her boy looking back at her said, without flinching.

"Good bye mother. May you enjoy your eternity as you look now; In Hell". Kim's daughter turned toward her step brother, telling him to "finish her." With that the boy jammed his foot on her chest, pushing Kim's body into a black hole that seemed to hook her bloody stump into a burning hell.

Curt looked on wondering if his fate would be the same.

Chapter 11 His Fate Is Known

Sickened by the fate of the woman named Kim, Curtis dropped to one knee, holding his stomach as he took in deep breaths. He felt dizzy and nauseas. Suddenly, he uncontrollably began to dry heave. The room was spinning, causing him to dry heave over and over. He stumbled to the ground and felt the cold floor on the side of his head. Curt attempted to not move, which helped decrease the spinning of the room. His eyes closed with both hands around the back of his neck attempting to massage away the dizziness. The dizziness turned to a migraine where the pain was only eased by his immobility. After lying on the floor, fighting the pains in his head, Curt passed out for hours.

Curt awoke by a familiar sound. With his eyes still shut and his arm over his eyes, he thought about the dream he thought he was having. Still wiped out from the violent thrashing caused from his nausea and dizziness, Curt laid there attempting to get more energy. He turned his head and could barely muster the strength to open his eyes, when he heard the sound again. It was a baby crying. He opened his eyes about halfway and realized he hadn't just dreamed his situation. He began to think of Kim and how she was savagely abused by her aborted children. Curt knew the sound of the crying baby was his and his fate was upon him.

He stumbled up to his knees before lifting himself completely up. His hands on his thighs, he straightened his knees until they locked straight. He then raised his arms to his hips as he straightened his back, bending it backwards, in an attempt to muster some strength in his body. With a deep sigh, Curt was prepared to face the music. Curt had begged his girlfriend not to have an abortion, but she still did, because she felt they were too young. Curt knew that they were too young, but losing his unborn child would be worse. Finally, after hours, days and weeks of soul searching on what to do, Curt gave his blessing to his girlfriend. Not that he had any choice in the matter; her mind was already made up. He tried to put her mind to peace. His old girlfriend went through with the abortion. They're relationship didn't last much longer.

Curt regretted giving his blessing. He had thought about what life would have been like with his lost child. Curt would constantly picture his unborn child with his two children. He knew there would have been a huge age gap between them of at least 16 years. He pictured his unborn daughter holding her sister and brother. Curt always felt it would have been a little girl born to him. He didn't know why, but always felt this strong bond it was a girl. He also named her Angel. The name came to him at his daughter's school play. As he watched her on stage, he couldn't help thinking of the daughter he lost. As he seen his little angel on stage, it occurred to him that, this would have been the name of his aborted child. There wasn't many a day that passed by that he didn't think about his daughter Angel. Even when he told his children how much he loved them, Curt knew how precious life was and always wanted his daughter and son to know how deep he loved them. Curt loved each of his three children.

So in a bassinette, smothered in a very strong sunlight, he heard crying. Curt didn't care what would happen to him. He knew what he had to do. So he walked over to the crib and for the first time, seen his beautiful daughter. She wasn't a medical mess as he had seen hours before in the room with Mother Theresa. She was a healthy, beautiful little girl, with dark hair and beautiful blue eyes. Curt was able to notice her eyes, because the small cries had turned to fussing and finally a smile as she made contact with her daddy for the very first time. "My God, you're so beautiful, little girl. I just need to tell you," Curt leaned over the bassinette caressing the delicate cheek of his child, with his fingertips. "I have missed you, and loved you every single day, since I've known about you." Tears swelled up in his eyes. "I am so sorry" his voice deepening and cracking, "that I wasn't strong enough or mature enough to save you. I am so, so sorry."

Curt had waited 30 years for this moment. Without a concern for his own safety, especially after what he just witnessed, Curt leaned over and held the child in his arms tight against his chest. The feeling he felt from the child was a sense of trust and security. When Curt's daughter, Crystal, was a child, he tripped carrying her down the steps on his pant leg. Without concern for himself, he threw himself backwards, taking the entire brunt of the steps as he fell down with the child in hand. He wrapped the child with both his arms and held Crystal tight against his chest. At the end of his painful fall, he called to his then wife, who had heard the crash and ran to see what happened. Curt ended up with a sore back, a severely sprained ankle, and a bruised ego. Crystal was never any wiser as she slept through the whole experience, protected by her daddy's arms.

Now he held his first born for the first time in his arms. The jubilation of the first embrace, yet the sadness of missing all the years of sharing his love, hit him like a freight train. He cried and cried, just repeating to his child "I'm so sorry, so sorry, I love you so much."

Curt held the child in his arms as she began to fuss. Almost instinctively, Curt began to sway back and forth with her. He placed her head on his shoulder, leaning his head against hers and sang to her. "There's a kinda hush, all over the world tonight, all over the world you can hear the sound of daddy in love, if you know what I mean. Just the two of us, and nobody else in sight and nobody else just the two of us holding you tight..."

As he sang to her, he felt something wrapped around his neck. He looked at the child and noticed a change. The child was about four years old. "My daddy." Angel squeezed her arms around Curt's neck. "I love my daddy."

"I love you too, my Angel." Curt twirled her without any remnants of his earlier dizzy attack.

Angel's arms began to get heavier and heavier around Curt's neck. Angel had become heavier. "Dad, you can put me done now." Angel had become a fully grown woman in the arms of her father.

"Oh, you're so beautiful." Curt began to cry again. "You lost out on a life, because of me."

"It's okay, really." Angel attempted to console her father. She hugged her 5 ft 4 inch frame around him, turning her head, allowing her auburn hair to shine in the light. "I want to tell you something. I would have been like all the other unborn had it not been for your love. I felt your love every day. I knew a long time ago, that I didn't just have a father, but I had a dad."

Curt smiled, but it vanished away quickly. "I'm no better than the woman who was tortured, by her children. I deserve the same fate."

Angel calmly stated "that woman never cared for her children. You have always cared about all your children, even me, especially me. God knows, we are not perfect. Everyone on earth has sins. God will forgive your sins. My life was lost before it began, but you have prayed and

thought about me every day. Others, who show no
recourse, will pay the ultimate price. The woman, Kim,
never gave a damn about life. Now she suffers the
ultimate punishment. Eternity in Hell." Angel wrapped
her arm around her father and began walking, almost
helping Curt along. There are many, like me waiting to
meet their parents. Many women have given up on a life
growing inside them, but have suffered the emotional
trauma of realizing what they had done. They can't
change things, but God allows a second chance. Some
earn it, like you dad, while others, like that Kim lady, do
not."

"What about your mother, what's her fate" a somber Curt
questioned.

"Deep down you would want her to burn in Hell, but that
was for breaking your heart." Angel laughed, trying to
snap her dad out of his doldrums. "Honestly, for the first
few years, I didn't think she come around. Then after her
first child was born, it bothered her, real bad. She never
told anyone that it bothered her. One night, she woke up
and just cried and cried. No dif'rent than you."

"Your mom was pressured to have an abortion. Everyone
told her we were too young." Curt pulled his hair back
giving it a tug as if trying to settle his own thoughts in his
head. "We talked about it. I never wanted her to have it.
However, I felt it was her decision, being it was her body. I
could have fought harder, look at you. You're beautiful,

intelligent, and funny. You know you get those traits from me." Curt smiled. "We both missed out on you."

"...and you both would have ended up hating each other. Where would I be? I'd be bouncing back and forth between the two of you."

"...and I would have loved every moment with you. In a way, I have always loved every moment with you. "Curt reached out and hugged Angel again only to push her, an arm's length away to stare into her eyes. "I have always loved you."

"I know, dad, I know." A smile on Angel's face told Curt they were going to be okay. "So, dad, tell me about my little brother and sister."

"They're awesome..." Curt's face lit up as he was able to talk to his daughter about her little sister and brother. They talked for hours walking, when suddenly they realized they were outside in desert like conditions.

As the two walked they noticed in the distance a black line. As they walked closer, the line turned in to many lines. "What is that?" Angel asked, looking concerned.

"Something tells me we're gonna find out sooner than later. Let's keep walking."

It wasn't long before they could finally make out, what was in front of them. They didn't like what they saw.

Chapter 12 Cross Country

"Jes-us Christ" as Curt's mouthed dropped as he realized what he was looking at. "There must be thousands and thousands of them."

"Thousands of what?" Angel asked, turning toward her father, before looking out again.

"Crosses. C'mon let's hurry up."

Soon, Curt and Angel began with a brisk walk, that evolved into a jog and finally a full blown sprint, the closer they came to the crosses. In the distance Curt could see each cross had a body attached to it. He also seen a small group of people assembled by the cross that seen to be in the front and center of all the crosses. "Do you think the people in front are dangerous?" as Angel grabbed her father's hand as they both abruptly stopped.

Thinking for a moment with his hands on his knees, Curt realized he was barely winded from their run. He hadn't felt this in shape since his days of running marathons. "I think were okay" as he stood straight up. "I think if they were a threat, we would have had a problem already."

Curt was right. As the two were just about to the reach the small crowd, the small crowd began lowering the cross gently to the ground. As the two approached the group of eight, the group seemed to split evenly, allowing Curt and Angel to walk right towards the cross. "Jesus Christ" Curt again said.

"Now what's wrong" Angel quizzing her father.

"No it's Jesus Christ. It's really him." Curt felt in awe of his presence.

"Help us get him off this cross." A strong late thirty something male stated with urgency. "Find something to remove these spikes from his hands and feet."

"Just open the wounds more and pull the hands over the spike. It will be the quickest way." A German accented man in his early thirties walked to the top of the cross and shook the hand back and forth, forcing screams of pain from Christ.

"Dad, what are you doing? This isn't a cow you're butchering. Stop!" The first man walked towards the man he called his dad, though the one called dad looked years younger, to prevent him from causing anymore pain.

Suddenly a third man grabbed the first man by the shoulder and stopped him in his tracks. Again, a German accent came from the largest of the three men. "Your dad knows what he is doing, Bill. Leave him alone."

"Bill? Dad is that you?" Curt looking over and realizing it was his father in his youth, before Curt was even born.

Curt wasn't sure who the man was holding back his father, but he recognized the man, trying to release Jesus was his grandfather. "Grandpa?"

"What are you doing here, already? Never mind, we'll talk later." Bill Jr. was shocked to see his son. "We have to save these people."

With a final scream, the hand of Jesus was brutally removed from the cross. Jesus immediately clutched his hand to his chest and he embraced for another painful removal of his left hand. Curt's grandfather struggled to get the second hand off the cross. The man, who was holding Curt's dad, released him and told him "Pull his feet out. I'll get his hand." The man looked at Curt's grandpa and calmly stated, "I got this Bill, go help your son." He forcibly tore the hand up, causing the hand to be ripped, causing the last two fingers to dangle, by his wrist. Jesus, again, screamed. "Forgive me, I am sorry to have hurt you."

Jesus held his hands against his chest and with a prayer "Please, give me the strength to heal myself, so I may be able to help others heal. I know father that you need us, but we need you more. We will always need your love and compassion you have for us. Please forgive our sins, so we may someday glow in the power of your light." With a flash of light, Jesus moved his hands away from his chest and they were healed. "Please remove, my feet quickly, so I may help you help the others." This time no cries rang out as Jesus' feet were freed from cross. With a touch of his hands, his feet were soothed and the damaged repaired by the will of God.

"Let's get the others off the crosses; we don't have a lot of time." Bill Jr. spoke to his dad "Joe, should we break in teams?" Bill turned to the larger gentleman, requesting his advice.

"No, we will work together, to free as many as we can, then have the ones we freed begin working as teams." Joe turned to Jesus bowing his head "With all due respect, will you be able to heal them all?" glancing around at the thousands of crosses.

"With the help of my father and your good souls, I will have the strength to heal."

Joe bowed in respect to Jesus. Joe was a very good man who was best friends with Bill Sr. The two had come from Germany to escape Nazi persecution. They left riches to start over in America. Both Joe and Bill respected each other and respected each other's opinions. Both stood up for each other. They were both proud men, who believed in always doing what was right. However, they both ruled with a firm hand, as Bill Jr. was on the back hand of many of these broken rules.

Once when Bill Jr. was five, he marched in a German parade with his dad on his left and Joe to his right. He was dressed in a green velour ledor hausen, as was his father

and his Uncle Joe. Joe wasn't related but because of the
bond between him and his dad, and the fact Joe lived with
his family, he was always Uncle Joe. There was not one
person more reliable than Uncle Joe. The three walked
proudly, Bill Jr. kicking his knees up high as he walked,
which was his way of honoring his dad and uncle. Being
five years old he didn't understand the ramifications of
walking in the German day parade. This was 1937, Hitler
in power in Germany and German Americans were being
ridiculed. The Schmidt's were not exempt from this
ridicule. This was demonstrated by a Nazi symbol being
painted on their house when they were at church. When
they came home from church and spotted the symbol on
the house, Bill was sickened by the thought of it. He loved
and missed his country, but despised the ruling party. Joe
told Bill "Take the family in the house. I will take care of
this mess."

Bill Jr., was unaware of all the angry people yelling at the
Germans parading down Main St. So as he walked
proudly, he turned with a smile on his face, first looking at
his Uncle Joe, who glanced down at Bill and gave him a
look of acknowledgement. Bill turned to his dad, who kept
his eyes looking straight ahead, with a very stern look on
his face. Bill looked straight ahead and march as proudly
as he could, lifting each leg as if he was lifting them higher
and higher with every step. Bill turned his head when he
heard a man yell "HEY KID". As his head turned to the
right, a sharp pain was felt in the left frontal lobe of his

forehead. Bill fell to the ground, from the rock that was thrown at him. Joe stopped and shielded the young boy as he scanned the ground to see who threw the rock. Bill was on his knees and began to cry. His father grabbed him hard under the shoulder and flung him back to his feet and yelled at Bill under his breath "Don't you dare cry. Do not give these people the satisfaction of you crying. If you cry, I will give you something worse to cry about at home."

Bill knew his father meant what he said. It took all his strength not to cry. His little body shook in fear, not only from being hit by the rock, but also from his father. He marched, lifting each foot as if it had concrete on them. He struggled through the parade, making it to the end. Joe picked him up and carried him, instead of letting him walk home, at the displeasure of Bill Sr. When they got home, Joe took a cold rag and cleaned the small cut on the forehead that had already swelled and was turning black and blue. With Bill Sr. watching and in agreement with Joe, Joe told Jr. "Today, you became a man. Today you learned what family is about. When one of us hurts, we all hurt. You may feel the sting of the stone, but I promise you we will always stick together. I will take care of healing this wound." Joe looked and Bill Sr. "Only I will take care of this, understood?" Bill Sr. shook his head in acknowledgement to Joe's intentions. Bill Jr. thought his Uncle Joe was talking about the wound to his head. Bill Sr. knew he was talking about the wound to their hearts that would only be handled with Joe's strong arm of justice.

That night Joe walked into O'Neill's tavern and confronted five men who were tossing the rocks. Before they could say a word to Joe, two of them had already had their smug looks wiped off their face. Two more tried in a valiant effort to jump Joe, only to find their heads banging together, like a Three Stooges movie. Only they also found Joe's shoes smashing against their body. The fifth guy just pleaded pathetically. Joe felt that disgrace was worse than a beating. "We are German. We are proud to be German. We hate what we see happening in our country. But most of all, we are Americans. You mess with one of us, you mess with us all. I will guard the Schmidt's, they are good people. Good German Americans. I am not of afraid of you. We are not afraid of you. If you want a fight, I will give you a fight. I will give you your wish. However, I wish for peace." Joe looked around the bar and no one said a word.   No one ever bothered them again.

Hours seem to turn to days and days possibly into weeks, as the crosses came down one by one. Smaller groups formed helping bring down 2, then 4, then 8, then 16 as the one small group became many. Soon, hundreds of groups turned to possibly thousands, forming a human chain of compassion for each soul waiting in angst for their new found freedom. The more they saved and the more Christ healed, the bigger and stronger the group became. Each group worked until every final soul was saved from crucifixion.

"Nice job son." Bill Jr. turned to his son, placing his hand on his shoulder, before embracing him in a hug. "What are you doing here? What happened?"

"I guess it was my time, that's all" Curt replied. "You look good dad."

"Thanks. Sorry if I didn't seem a little more excited to see you earlier. I mean Jesus, it was Jesus. I didn't mean to be short with you. Amazing place; your grandfather looks better than me." Bill laughed "It's great to see you son, well not great, 'cause your dead. I'd rather not see you, 'cause that means you're alive, I rather miss you than see you. But it is really great to see you, son."

"Have you been watching too many Green Acres reruns up here, dad, or should I call you Mr. Kimball?" Curt smiled at his father's indecisiveness, referencing a character from the 60's television show that they watched together.

"How are my grand children? You shouldn't be here, your kids need you."

"My kids are strong. Crystal reminds me of mom and my son, Colin reminds me a lot of you. They are great kids. "Curt paused for a moment and turned toward Angel "Dad, this is Angel my oldest daughter."

"I wondered when I would meet you. My, my, you're a beautiful girl" Bill hugged Angel and turned back to Curt.

"You had a hard time with what happened with this little girl. You must be grateful to finally be with her."

Curt smiled and grabbed his daughter away from his father, kissed her on the cheek, as he hugged her. "I haven't felt love like this, since my other two were born. I guess another one snuck through the chains and barbed wire around my heart."   Curt proudly hugged Angel.

"Enjoy your moment with her son, 'cause we need to get going."

"Go, where?" Curt asked.

"HELL, my boy, I thought you could figure that out yourself."

Chapter 13 The Game Plan

Curt looked confused as his father smirked, his lips touching slightly in front as his teeth glistened off the sides of his mouth. "Boy could I go for a smoke now." Bill placed his hand by his mouth mimicking a long drag of a cigarette. "You think I would have lost that urge here."

"Where are we going?" Curt asked again.

"No more time for games. Bill, Curt, you come with me. We have a lot to talk about and figure out. We have a war here that needs to be won." Bill Sr. stated as he came over to the discussion between his son and grandson. "I will explain it all to you, both. Joe has a plan that I think will work."

So the two Bills, Joe, Angel, and Curt walked over to Jesus. Joe kneeled down in front of Jesus, lowering his head in respect of his savior. "You are blessed to be the son of God. I should not ask anymore of you than you have already done. You have healed thousands from their injuries from their crucifixions. You have laid down your life, so we may have a better life. I do wish to ask a favor of you. I know you are a peaceful man, yet we need your guidance in order to succeed. I ask that you allow us to fight, to win back our world and to bring joy and happiness into the heavens."

"The only way to win this war is through love." A humbled Jesus lifted the head of Joe, "please, do not kneel in front of me. I am a man like, you. You have presented yourself with dignity throughout your life. I should be kneeling to you. I possess the power to heal, I possess the power to preach, and I possess the power to love. However, I do not possess the power to fight as it against my beliefs. You, Joe, are not afraid to fight, you are not afraid to lead and take control. You know what you must do and I will pray for you here. So I give you my blessing to gather an army of men to fight your war. The world from where we all came is crippled. Men keep trying to figure out the universe, men attempting to learn the secrets of God. The more they learn, the more their hunger cries for more. The more they learn about the secrets of God, they start to believe they are God. The more they believe they are God, the less they believe in God. They won't be satisfied until their thirst of knowledge is quenched. They have become more and more cynical. If man could only show patience, all their answers about the universe would someday be answered in heaven. However, without their belief in the heavens, has weakened the heavens. We must gain back the heavens and place God back as our spiritual leader."

"So I will build an army from the men who wish to fight with me?"

"I will fight next to you..." Bill Sr. confidently shouted out.

"...and I next to you, dad!" Jr. stood next to his father backing him up.

"No, no, no..." Jesus interrupted. You must find God. You have been brought here to find him, in the far depths of Hell, where he was taken by Lucifer. Joe must prepare Heaven for God again, but it will take courage, fortitude, and teamwork to succeed. It will especially take love. You will need the love that one will lay on the line for a loved one. The four of you" as Jesus alluded to the two Bills, Curt, and Angel, "have been brought together for one reason only. That is to find God. If you do not succeed in your quest, God help our father and God help us all."

"I have always stood next to Joe. I can help him." Sr. respectfully answered.

"No, not this time Bill" Joe responded with pride in the fact they Sr. would be willing to place himself in harm way to protect Joe. "We have always looked out for each other. Now we must trust each other to complete our destinies. We may not be standing next to each other in this fight, but we will be holding each other throughout."

Silence came over the group as they knew the word of Jesus would guide them. "Then we shall go to Hell and come back successful! WE WON'T FAIL!" Sr. broke the silence causing an eruption of cheers from the thousands listening all around.

"I shall prepare an army to take back to Heaven. I promise you, I won't fail." Joe placed his hand on the shoulder of his best friend as they embraced, by giving each other two hard smacks on the back that seemed more painful than friendly. "You have always been there for me Bill. I will prepare the Heavens for the coming of our Lord." With that statement, the two men shook hands and placed their left hand on each other's forearm, giving each other a warmer embrace that comforted both.

"I will stay and pray for us. I will pray for our sins. I will pray for your safe return." Jesus placed his hands on the shoulders of the two men, as the warmth of love overpowered the small group, giving them the confidence for success. Both men bowed their heads to Jesus, before looking back at each other, nodding in approval to their quest.

"Let's go." Sr. turned to his army of three and headed in a direction opposite that of Joe. Jesus knelt with men, women, and children as they prayed for the savior of all souls. Joe gathered men, willing to risk their heavenly lives on the mission in hand.

"What's our game plan?" Curt asked his grandfather. "What do we do when we get there?"

"Too many questions, we will know when it is time." Sr. sternly told his grandson.

"Just be ready and listen to what we tell you." His father chimed in.

Angel leaned on her dad "don't worry dad, we'll know."

The reassurance by everyone didn't seem to help Curt, as he felt he was the only one in the dark. As they walked, the skies began to blacken. The land became like lava rock as earthquakes started to shake the ground. Lightning flashed across the skies. The group came across a rickety old bridge that was missing boards that crossed a swollen river near a waterfall. Senior placed his hand gently on Angel's and guided her to the other side of the bridge. Junior and Curt started to cross. Curt shook as he felt petrified of his surroundings. He hadn't felt like this in years. The imagery made him feel like he was in a peaceful dream that suddenly went into a nightmare. He froze for a moment, feeling his legs quiver beneath him. In a voice of confidence and said in a mild tone, "it's okay son, I will always be there for you. " Curt looked at his father, somewhat bewildered.

"The last time you spoke to me like that, was after Angel..." his voice cracking as Curt fought for the words to come out, "I mean after I came home, after I was too late to help her." Curt spoke of the circumstances of Angel's premature demise.

"I love you son, just remember that. I always have and always will. C'mon let's get over this bridge."

Carefully, they crossed over the bridge, when suddenly, a frayed rope snapped and the bridge plummeted down knocking both men off their feet and onto the boards of the bridge. The bridge fell about 6 inches just enough to give the men a good scare, before it settled. Curt and Jr. looked at each other and laughed nervously as they slowly got back to their feet. Curt was almost at the end of the bridge, when the rope had snapped. Curt had found himself turned and was face to face with his father after their mini free fall. They looked at each other and Bill shook his head in disbelief as he stated to Curt, "Let's get moving." Curt turned, but as he stepped on the first board back from his fall, the board snapped under his foot, causing a large hole ready to swallow him in a flash. Instinctively, Bill thrust his body forward, extending his arms, and pushed Curt forward over the hole as he stumbled safely to the other side. The pressure on the bridge from Bill's sudden outburst snapped the frayed ropes from the side. Bill's foot landed in front of the hole that had been formed from Curt. Bill held the rope on the side for balance. The bridge collapsed and Bill made a valiant effort to jump to the other side. Curt reached back as he reached for his father's arms, but only their index fingers touched as Curt watched his father disappear down the gorge for which they were crossing. As quickly as Bill Jr. was back in Curt's life, he was gone. "NNNNNNNNNNNOOOOOOOOOOO. DAD, DAD, DAD!" Curt cried out as he looked for a way down to attempt a rescue of his father.

His grandfather grabbed his arm and pulled him back to his feet. "It's too late, he's gone."

"He can't be. DAD. I just got him back in my life."

"He's back in God's hands. God allowed you to be with your father, again. He allowed me to be with my son, again. I know we will be together, again. You must stay strong. Your father would want that. We must move on." Curt just stood there, when his grandfather grabbed his arm in anger as he also lost his son, but knew there was no time to waste. "If you believe in God, you will see your father again." Bill Sr. stated as he calmed down and released the grip on Curt's arm. "We don't know what is ahead of us, but we must stay strong. If we do not, we will fail and let everyone down. So if we want to see our loved one's again, we must go. We must." Bill placed his arm around his grandson hugging him, before he started to walk away from the edge of the cliff.

Feeling as if he was just abandoned by his father, Curt turned toward his grandfather and daughter, before turning back one last time. "I love you, dad." Angel took hold of Curt's hand as they proceeded to follow Bill Sr., to the depths of Hell. They weren't even at Hell's doorstep, yet they all felt the pain of what Hell was all about.

Chapter 14 Slot In Hell

Curt was embraced by Angel as he was still hurting from the loss of his dad. His grandfather walked a few steps ahead, periodically looking back. "There is a greater plan in place that we must believe in. Your father, my son, has not died again, but has risen to a higher calling. This is what I believe and you must too."

"He is right you know. I had to believe a better day would come for me and it has," Angel softly spoke, "deep down you know a better day has come for your dad. We must believe a better day will come for us all, otherwise why are we here?"

Curt stopped walking for a moment, turned toward his daughter and stared directly into her eyes. "Your right, otherwise I wouldn't be with you now."   The two embraced and began walking faster to catch up to Bill Sr. who had just kept moving ahead.

They walked through a desert, feeling the hot sun on their skin. The winds began whipping up, making the sand sting against their bodies. "Keep walking, never surrender," Bill yelled over the howling winds. Soon the winds and sand picked up in their relentless attempt to slow down the three family members. With their heads down and arms interlocked with each other, the three struggled onward. Soon the winds died down and the sand fell back to the ground, showing the three the exotic world of Las Vegas. The strip was hustling with people looking to gamble, looking for sex, and just looking for a good time. Others were looking to rob, were begging for food and drink, and others were performing in an effort to earn a few dollars not to go home, but to gamble it back away in the casinos. Basically, it was Las Vegas in 2012. As they opened the casino door of the Venetian, the interior was not what Curt had envisioned it to be. When he was alive he stayed at the Venetian and remembered the beautiful gardens and artwork that lined the interior. He remembered the high ceilings which allowed light to shine in, giving the casino a very pleasant place to visit. However, the interior here was not inviting but seedy. The ceilings were lower as they were covered with maroon carpeting that matched the carpeting on the floor. The room smelled of stale cigarettes and mold. Slot machines were lined up in a straight line on both sides, leading them directly, to a cashier at the other end of the casino floor.

The three walked down the middle of the aisle, as some people pulled the handles of the slot machines, some banged on the buttons in front, and others hitting the maximum play over and over. The people played hoping for a big hit, but every pull of the handle, every hit of the button, each was giving away part of their soul. The three watched as a balding man made his last bet of his soul. Three devil forks appeared in the window. A voice came through the machine "You won an eternity of free plays."

The man jumped in excitement of his luck. He gave up his soul, bet received what he always wanted. With an eternity of free plays, he would reap millions, possibly billions, trillions, eventually googles of money. He began hitting the max play button for the results would be faster. His first spin, lost. His second lost. After a hundred spins he lost. Frustrated, he pushed the max button faster looking for the big payday. Soon it was obvious that there would never be a big payday. Not even a small payday. Not even a cherry would appear with a couple of credits. He cried out in frustration, but he kept hitting the button, because it was due to hit. The three walked away as the broken down man had been forced into an eternity of self destruction. The slot machine taunted him making it unbearable for the man. The machine only handed out the pain of hopelessness. The man succumbed to this, however, just one more try...

Chapter 15 My Soul To Keep

The trio headed past the slot machine and headed toward the cashier's cage. "Where do you think you're headed?" A hunched man with crippled hands demanded a response from the three. The lifting of the bags of money and the endless counting of casino chips had left him irritable and impatient. His pale, wrinkled skin from lack of sunlight and excessive amounts of cigarette smoke seemed to blend his body with the money bags behind him. "Where you're headed, there is no free ride. You gotta pay first," as he continued to speak through his yellowed broken teeth and rusty cage separating him from the outside world.

"Where we are headed is none of your business." Sr. spouted back. "Keep walking you two. Don't let this sad sack of sorrows intimidate you."

"NO ONE PASSES THROUGH HERE WITHOUT RELEASING THEIR SOULS TO ME. NO ONE!!!"

"Oh you have quite the temper, now don't ya? We are so scared!" Sr. mocked the wrinkled old bag by shaking his hand in front of him in teasing the caged animal.

"Give me YOUR SOUL."

"How 'bout I give you a kick in the ass?" smirking and taunting the man to the point he began throwing chips at Sr. from behind his cage. Sr. bent over and picked a few up, "Thank you for the tip," and placed them in his pocket.

"Give me my chips back and your soul, NOW."

"I tell you vhat…" Sr.'s German accent slipping out, "I shall give your chips to the people outside. You vill never see them again."

"Don't you do it, don't you do it," as Sr. motioned Curt and Angel to follow him back toward the street. "You're bluffing, I know you're bluffing." The three kept walking, as Sr. pulled out a coin and flipped it on the floor in front of him, sending all the slot players to dive on the floor after it. "NNNNNOOOOO, COME BACK, PLEASE GIVE ME MY COINS, I WILL LET YOU PASS."

The three turned around and headed back toward the cage. The old man in the cage was panting from panic, his mouth covered from white foam from spitting as he spoke. "Why, don't I believe you?" Bill Sr. shouted back.

"I will, just, well I need my coins."

"You need to let us pass."

Still panting out of breathe "You can only pass if you give me your soul and give me my chips."

"You vant your chips? How badly do you vant them?"

"We will gamble for the chips. I know you will bet your souls and my chips on a game. If I win, I get your souls and my chips back. If you win, I will let you pass, no soul to take, my chips would be yours."

Bill thought for a moment before responding, "We will play a game and if I win, you will let us pass, but if you win, we give up our souls and your petty chips? That sounds reasonable."

Curt and Angel looked at each other in disbelief, before turning back to their grandfather who was now standing in front of the cage. The old man looked at him and smiled through his still heavy breathing. "So you will play a game of blackjack? How 'bout poker? Heh, how 'bout a game of war?"

"First you agree that I choose the game. Second, you agree to play fair. Finally, if I win, we pass. If I lose, our souls and your precious chips are yours. Agreed?"

Pondering for a moment, "Okay, you choose the game. I will agree to the terms if you give me my chips."

"I will give you one, you can win the rest. Do we have a deal?"

"Yes, yes now give me my chip," as the old soul taker reached his bony hands outward from his cage, where Sr. handed him one chip. Pressing the chip against his chest, he then threw it onto the bags piled behind him. He then reached for a new deck of cards and opened them at the window. He showed Sr. all 52 cards were there. He then began to mix them and shuffle them. "Do you wish to cut them?"

"No, I trust you. You seem like a man of your word."

"Oh, I am. So, what game do you wish to play?"

"It's a simple game. I will guess the color of the card, either red or black. If I guess half the deck or more correctly, then we can pass. If I guess less than half correct, you win. Fair, enough?"

"Yes, yes, I will accept your bet. My pile will be to my left of the cards you guess wrong. If you are right, I will place them to my right. Let's begin. Is the first card black or red?"

"Black."

The first card flipped was the 4 of diamonds. "WRONG. You are down 1. Now what is your guess?"

Pausing for a moment, Sr. responded "Black...again."

"TOO BAD, WRONG AGAIN. Choose again," as the 9 of hearts was displayed.

Acting nervous, Bill Sr. looked over at Curt and Angel, "What do you guys think?" They both shook their heads in disbelief, for they did not want to be wrong either.

Turning back to the cage "Black, it's got to be a black card."

"Jack of hearts!" The old man was laughing loudly.

Sr. rubbed his hands in disbelief as he shouted "Black, black, black" on the next three cards. But the cards came out as the 2 of diamonds, Ace of diamonds, followed by the 6 of hearts. "You're cheating me, aren't you?" Sr. accused the old man.

"Don't need to, don't have to. Your just not lucky I guess," laughing loudly as Curt and Angel looked concerned about their fates.

"Just quit grandpa. Let's get outta here." Curt nervously reacted to the situation.

"You quit and I win, automatically."

"He's right," Sr. acknowledged. "I have never gone back on a deal. A deal is a deal. Win or lose. Please show me a black card."

"8 of clubs," a little jubilation left the caged man. However, he was still up 6 to 1. "You were bound to guess one right."

"Black"

"Jack of diamonds! 7 to 1." The old man snickered, "try again?"

"Black"

"King of spades. 7 to 2."

"Black"

"2 of clubs," the old man slapped the card into the right pile.

"Black"

Then it occurred to the old man. All Sr. had to do was guess black each time and he would win, since half the deck was black. "You tricked me, this game is not fair. You cheated."

"You agreed to it and it is fair. You're winning aren 't you? I don't know if I will guess red or black. I'm thinking maybe I might change it up a little."

"So you want red?"

"Nah, black."

"King of diamonds."

"Again, black;" The old man flipped the card knowing Sr. got the best of him. Like one of the slot players, he hoped Sr. would change from black to red and be wrong. But black was the choice through the deck. With three cards remaining, Sr. was down 26 to 23. "Hmmm, three cards left, I gotta be right on all three, so I'll guess black, black, and black." The old man flipped all three at once exposing the final three black cards. He placed his head down and hit a button on the side with his right hand, opening an elevator door. The three jumped in and the door closed in front of them.

"Where did you learn that trick?" Curt's amazement glowing as he was shocked by his grandfather's ingenious smart play and quick thinking. "You had me going for awhile."

"Old bar game. You lose to it once and never lose to it again. You wait for your moment to use it on someone else. Today was that day." Bill smiled as he pushed the down button on the elevator. The button was marked Hell. "Hang on I think this might be a rough ride." The three gripped the gold handles on the side as they felt the elevator descend downward slowly. Suddenly the elevator released from its cable and flew down so rapidly the three found themselves hanging onto the handles with their feet on the ceiling of the elevator. They knew there landing may be their last.

Chapter 16 666

"DAD, we're gonna die aren't we?" Angel screamed as she reached out her hand towards Curt that had slipped off the railing. Curt let go of his right hand and grabbed Angel's hand and held it tight.

Curt thought they were in real trouble and weren't going to make it. He needed to placate Angel, because no matter how bad the situation, his daughter shouldn't be upset. "Look at me." Curt calmly affirmed, "We will be okay, just have faith." Curt loosened his grip on Angel's hand and gave it a slight squeeze. "I've fallen like this earlier and I'm okay. Just think happy thoughts un..." The elevator began to slow down as rapidly as it sped up, hurling the three family members hard to the floor. They laid on the floor until the elevator came to a complete stop. A bell rang and the elevator doors opened. "I didn't expect to face plant! I knew it be rough, but that hurt." They all stood up, looked at each other as they realized they were in Hell and that there would be no turning back.

Straight ahead were the Gates of Hell. The gates were wide open as nobody or no thing was guarding them. The gates seemed to invite you in, but surely wouldn't want you to get out. When the three looked around they noticed the only direction they would be able to go was straight ahead about 666 steps. They slowly began to walk towards the gates with Sr. leading the way with Angel and Curtis trailing close behind. They looked over to their right, being barely 20 yards outside the elevator doors. Here, they saw people hanging on ropes from trees, none of them dead and all gasping for air. The sound of the little bit of air being released from their lungs was sickening. To their left, people screamed in agony from the constant friction of copulation their genitals felt. Rapists screamed in pain, having their penises raw from constant use. Women, who were prostitutes screamed in anguish, at they were tortured by the raw abrasions they suffered inside them. Curt realized they were not all prostitutes as he spotted a familiar face. He heard the cries of "Please, stop, please. Why are you doing this to me?" Curt looked over to see Kim, the woman who had multiple abortions. Feeling an urge to help, he turned to his grandfather.

"I know she did wrong, but this is wrong, it's worse than wrong. We have to help her."

"The pain those children went through? I had to endure it too. You would rather help her." Angel cried "I waited years for this?"

"No, no, no, it's not like that. I love you and have always loved you. I wouldn't want to see you in pain or anyone else. It's just…"

"...The way it is. I've heard enough from both of you. This is not your fight. You have each other, she" Bill pointed to the woman, "determined her own outcome, not either one of you."

"He's right Angel." Curt looked directly at Angel so he could avoid contact with Kim, "I'm just so sorry I couldn't save you. I couldn't help you. I am no better than her."

"Then why are you here and she's there? She chose her outcome and you chose yours." Angel wiped her eyes as Curt held her tight.

"You didn't deserve your fate, Angel. It was my fault I wasn't strong enough." Curt was still holding her tight, his hand on her head as she wrapped her arms around his neck. "We, okay?" Curt tilted his head to see the look on his daughter. A small smile appeared on his lips. Angel smiled back as she nodded in approval.

"Things will only get worse, is my feeling," Sr. stated, "We are barely 5 feet out in Hell and already this place is affecting us. We must stay strong or we will never succeed."

Chapter 17 My Little Angel

Curt knew his grandfather was right. "Let's move on," in a reluctant yet determined voice.

The three headed down a rocky path that glowed red. Molten lava flowed like a river in front of them forcing them to carefully cross rocks barely above the flow. They reached a plateau that left them looking into the darkness. They could not see above or below. They slowly carried on not knowing if the next step would be their last. Soon the darkness completely surrounded them. Sr. stepped first, followed by Curt then Angel. "Be careful, I feel slimy rocks ahead," as Sr. warned the other two.

The three ventured unaware of their surroundings.   They felt at first stickiness on the rocks. Then the stickiness turned to wetness. The wetness was warm and clearly was thicker than water. A red light exposed itself ahead. As they made it to the light, they realized they were covered in blood that was seeping through the rocks. They looked at their hands and wiped them on their clothing, not saying a word, as there wasn't much they could do about the situation.

Bill gasped as he was caught off guard for what he was looking at. Curt and Angel looked up at Sr. and then followed his line of vision. Angel screamed before ducking her head in Curt's shoulder. Curt felt sick. All three had prepared themselves for the unexpected gory sights, but no one was prepared for what was in front of them.

Looking at a blood river flowing in front of them would have been horrific enough. To see bodies gasping for air, spitting out blood, was beyond any inhumane treatment they could have imagined. Sr. instinctively, reached in to grab the outstretched hand of a man gasping and coughing for a breath. The man's eyes were wide open in fear. As the man spit out blood, he attempted to cry for help, but only death gurgles were emitted.

Curt hung onto Bill's right arm and shunned Angel away from the river with his left hand. The current of the river looked strong, as waves flowed over the open mouths of the struggling souls. Instead of white caps forming like in water, the three witnessed black caps form from the darkness of the blood.

Sr. gripped the hand of the struggling man, who was now jerking his body like a fish. Sr. and Curt pulled back dragging the man onto the rocky shore. The bottom half of the man was missing. His hacked up, crippled body, with his intestines flowing out, forced the three to unconsciously step back when the intestines began to move like snakes. The mutilated man's mouth was moving, unable to speak words. Sr. moved down, placing his hands on the side of the man's face to reassure him somehow, everything would be okay. The deathly stare from the man to Sr., forced Sr. not to look him directly in the eyes, but towards the man's mouth where blood was pouring out of. The man's intestines took hold of the ground like suction cups and stiffened as they threw the man back into the river. Curt grabbed a hold of his grandfather, saving him from falling into the river with the man, as one the torn intestines wrapped around Sr.'s ankle, before falling back into the river. As the man coughed out the remaining blood from his throat, spewing the blood in front of him, he was able to say the words "help, me" before falling back head first into the red sea. His intestines stretched for a moment on the rocks before their suction released burying the man in the river.

"We can't save them," Sr. announced as he stood up from one knee. "It's not our quest, we must go on." Sr. pointed in a direction, without saying a word, with Curt and Angel following close by. The three walked for miles and miles when they heard a blood curdling roar ahead. A waterfall of blood flowed down from the rocks hundreds of feet above. There did not look to be anywhere to cross, as the three felt they may have headed in the wrong direction. There was nothing they could use to cross the river as it would have been too dangerous to try. "Maybe we can cross behind the falls." They headed towards the bottom of the cliff, where Sr. spotted an opening. "See," Sr. pointed, "we can cross here."

The rocks were completely covered with blood as they headed on behind the falls. However, at this point, they themselves were completely covered in blood. They made their way to the other side of the river, having to duck under a flow of blood that poured out like a fountain in the rock.

On the other side, was heavy brush that forced the three onto a very narrow walkway. As they walked they noticed the plants starting to move. The one plant struck Curt on the arm, little needles sticking him. He pulled back ripping his shirt and tearing the flesh of his skin trying to get this plant off of him. "Venus flytraps, run!" he screamed.

The three bolted down the path, dodging and ducking the snapping plants. Sr.'s leg was wrapped by a vine of the plant sending him down, head first on a rock, dazing him. Angel began kicking at the vine before reaching down and pulling it off Bill Sr.'s leg. Curt pulled Sr. up by lifting him under his arms and dragging him about 100 yards to safety. Angel followed them out. "Grandpa, you okay?" Curt laid him down on his back.

Sr. grimaced for a moment, shaking his head, before coming to his senses. "Thank you. Wow that hurts."

Curt helped him sit up. Sr. wrapped his arms around his knees, moving his neck up and down and side to side. "I'll be okay. How are you guys."

"Okay" Curt responded.

"We are good" Angel followed up with.

As Bill Sr. was getting back to his feet, Curt and Angel watched as he was somewhat groggy. What they should have been doing is watching the plants behind them. They thought they were a good distance away, but the vines on the plants were long and stretched out quietly. Sr. stood up bending his back, eyes closed, still moving his neck side to side. He opened his eyes, blinking a few times, as he squeezed the back of his neck, again closing his eyes. He reopened them relaxed, smiling before he dove back to the ground at Angel's feet. "ANGEL" he screamed turning Curt's attention toward her.

Sr. missed grabbing Angel as the vines of the plants wrapped around her legs and her arms sending her violently into the air. Curt ran after her screaming. He jumped up to reach her, but she was out of his reach. The plants then began to stretch her. She screamed as the vines pulled her body tight, until they tore her in two, before throwing he back, into the mouths of the hungry beast. Her blood sprayed onto the outreached hands of Curt. "NOOOOOO" he cried. "Why, why, why? My baby, my baby." Curt looked at his hands and rubbed them on his chest over his heart.

Sr. ran over, hugging him, trying to console him. "There must be a reason Curt, there must be a plan."

"I give up, I can't go on; I just can't do it anymore." Curt was despondent in grief.

"Don't let Angel be gone, without meaning. You can't do that to her." Sr. said crying. Curt looked at his grandfather, realizing this is the first time he ever seen him cry. "Go on for Angel, you must honor her by going on."

The two embraced, walking slowly, crying along the way.

Chapter 18 Pandora's Box

"WWWWHHHHHYYYYYY?" Curt let out a curdling scream. He dropped to his knees and stared at his hands, which remained full of blood.

"C'mon damnit, be strong. You owe it to Angel."

"I just got her back and I lost her. What kind of father am I? I couldn't save my child."

Sr. dropped to his left knee and placed his arm around Curt. With his left hand he gripped Curt's hands. "You are the best father. I ruled my children with a rod. It was the way then. You were there for your children. You were always there for Angel. Neither of us could save her. It happened too quickly. We must believe God has a plan. Now we are in Hell. Soon we will all be together in Heaven. If you don't believe what I am saying, then let's go back now, because there is no use in going on if you don't believe. Your father did not go in vain and neither will Angel." Curt looked at his grandfather, who looked younger than him, but was much wiser than Curt could ever imagine. "I don't believe it was an accident that we have all been brought together. I don't believe it was an accident we both lost a child. God has a plan and we must obey it." Sr. helped Curt back to his feet and the two began walking again.

As they walked Curt began to get angry. "No more, no more," he kept repeating under his breath. Curt had had enough feeling of pain and suffering in his life and now his afterlife. He was about to release his wrath on anyone or anything that got in his way.

Sr. took notice of Curt's anger, but said nothing. He allowed Curt to vent under his breath, but placed his hand over Curt's mouth "Shhh" when he spotted something moving by the jagged rocks straight ahead. Crouching lower so not to be seen, the two headed to the edge of the rocks and looked down at a crowd of people forming.

The crowd seemed to be getting larger. The noise level from the yelling and screaming became deafening. Soon a fight erupted between a man with a sword and one with a club, in the center of the mob. Without hesitation, the man with the sword swung mightily at the head of the man with the club. The clubbed man blocked the sword, by raising his club and swinging it to the right. The man with the sword screamed, his veins pulsating in the side of his neck. The crowd had formed a circle around the two, with people pushing them back in the middle as they stepped back. Again, the sword swung and the man with the club moved to the side, hitting a wall of people. He was pushed back, stumbling as he attempted to stay on his feet as he fell toward the other side of the crowd. He regained his balance just as the sword swung at him from his left. He ducked just as another crowd member attempted to push him toward the sword. That turned out to be unfortunate for that person. As the clubbed man ducked, the sword hit the man across the shoulder, lodging deep into the chest cavity. As the sword wielding man attempted to remove the sword, the man with the club, smashed down directly on the head, of the man with the sword, crushing his skull. The man with the sword went down to the ground, still hanging onto the lodged sword, bringing the member from the crowd down on the ground with him. The sworded man released one hand from his sword, placing it up to block the onset of the club. His eyes filled with fear as the club smashed by his hand and directly into his face. The clubbed man kept hitting and smashing his head until nothing was recognizable. Then he released a laugh as he began to do the same to the bystander with the sword in his chest. The crowd roared with approval as the two bodies were then dragged back to a bent up, rusting looking box that people were coming out of. The clubbed man smashed the head of the next person coming out of the box, blocking anyone from coming out. With his club he pushed the body back in the box and then proceeded to do the same with the now unrecognizable corpses he had dragged to this point. He pushed, smashed and crushed the two bodies until they were completely back into the box. He then proceeded to smash the box shut, not allowing anymore or anyone to come out again. "To Hell with Pandora's Box," he screamed. "I am now in charge of Hell and anyone who thinks otherwise will be put to death by me. No one comes and no one goes, without going through me!"

"Hail to Brutus," the crowd began to chant.

"What do we do now?" whispered Curt. "They will destroy us if we try to get through."

"Our mission is not complete, until we locate God." Sr. said quietly.

"But where is he, what does he look like. Is God in man's image?"

"I believe our vision of God is what we make of him. My vision is of God is from Michealango's Creation of Adam. I believe his vision is the correct vision. I also believe that God would be in the darkest depths of Hell. It will be there, he will be found.

Curt knew his grandfather was speaking from the heart. He knew their quest would be leading them into the darkest realms of Hell. The problem was getting there. Brutus dispatched groups of men in every direction, to bring back the men who have strayed away. A group was summoned in the direction of Bill and Curt.

"Now what do we do?" Curt looked at his grandfather and then back the way they came. He knew he couldn't go back. The two would need to fight.

"I want you to listen to me very closely. This is the only plan and you must follow it exactly, or everything we sought will be gone. I am going to challenge the man they call Brutus to a duel. You will hide behind those rocks," Sr. pointed back down the path they came, "and wait until I am in front of Brutus. At that time you will pass by the crowd and head farther down the journey. I know we are close, because the darkest depths of Hell are frozen, and I see fog straight ahead where the heat must be hitting the cold."

"Let me go instead of you, I..." Curt was cut off in mid sentence.

"Are you questioning my fighting ability? Do you question my strength? I can handle myself better than you. Now, there is no time. I have it already planned in my head. Now go behind those rocks." Sr. pushed Curt towards them, knocking him off balance.

"Be careful Grandpa. I love you." Curt reached out his hand towards his grandfather. His grandfather turned toward the oncoming party and reached back and gripped Curt's hand by the fingers and then released them as he stood up straight drawing attention to himself as he walked toward the search party. Curt scurried to hide behind the rocks his grandfather told him to go to.

"Brutus, Brutus, I have traveled a long way to challenge you're so called leader for the rights to run Hell," as Sr.

stood with his arms on his hips and chest out. "Take me to him, NOW!"

6 men with spears surrounded Sr. and walked him back towards the crowd. Two walked in front of him, one on each side of him, and two behind him. They all walked with their spears in the air, except for the two behind Sr., who kept jabbing him in his back just under his shoulder blades. They entered the crowd and Sr. was screaming, "Where is Brutus?" drawing attention and all eyes on him.

Curt then began to follow the rocky path until there were no more rocks to hide behind. At this point Curt waited until he seen his grandfather face to face with Brutus.

Laughing, "You challenge me, with no weapon to fight to the death?" Brutus felt amused. "Even I could not kill you now, as it would be too easy. Name your weapon and we shall fight with the weapon of your choice."

"I choose hand to hand combat."

"NOT AN OPTION" Brutus became upset, taking his club and landing a hard blow to the side of Sr.'s ribs. The sound of breaking ribs could be heard all the way back to where Curt was hiding.

Curt became angry and looked around for a weapon to help his grandfather. But then he remembered he needed to follow what his grandfather told him. With a sudden burst of energy, Curt ran toward the steam his grandfather has alluded to and buried himself deep within it, without anyone spotting him. There he listened.

"Give me a sword to fight you with." Bill Sr. grimaced in agony, grinding his teeth to help bear with the pain. Brutus smiled and walked to the crowd where he was handed to swords. He threw one at the feet of Sr. Bill Sr. bent over to pick it up as Brutus walked to the other end of the newly formed circle of people. Sr. picked up the sword and used it to balance himself, digging the tip of the sword into the dirt. "Come get me scum bag."

The smile left the face of Brutus. His eyes became red with anger. He lifted the sword as he ran toward Sr. The tip of Brutus blade was aimed right at the heart of Sr. Brutus ran toward him. Sr. reacted by dropping his blade to the ground and extending his arms as if being crucified. The sword penetrated the chest of Bill Sr. and expelled through his back. With his final breath, Sr. screamed "I love you, Curtis. Succeed!" Sr. dropped to his knees before collapsing to the ground.

Brutus screamed in ecstasy as he dragged Sr. to Pandora's box and stuffing his body inside.

The crowd chanted "Hail to Brutus".

Chapter 19 All The President's Men

Curt could not see, but knew what just occurred. His grandfather did not even fight back. All he did was cause enough of a commotion to buy Curt time to pass by the crowd. Curt realized he was now alone, again.

When Curt's journey began he walked in nothingness with no real sense of purpose. He could see forever, but had no mission ahead. Now, he could see nothing but his vision. His quest would need to be completed alone. It was the way.

Curt thought about what happened to his mom, his dad, his little girl, and now his grandfather. He stood in this steam bath wanting to scream, but knew he could not or he would be found. The steam was like a shower, washing the blood off of Curt. He began walking through the steam when it began to get cold, extremely cold. The steam began to diminish and he found himself staring in front of a cave, with large icicles precariously hanging from the top. He was able to see himself in the frozen water that had formed on the side of the cave. He noticed that he had no bloodstains on his body. He looked at his hands and realized the blood of Angel was gone. He had no evidence of her except a memory.

Curt swallowed hard, fighting back tears, as the lump in his throat seemed to grow. His heart ached, but he knew he had to forge onward. He walked, entering the opening passage of the cave. He wasn't fifty feet in when he noticed a figure frozen behind the ice. As he stared at the man, a vision appeared in the ice by the man. The image showed the man hurting a child sexually. The child cried for his mother, while the man laughed as the child's crying brought him extra enjoyment. Curt turned away sickened, feeling more heartache after seeing the pain in the young boy.

Curt sickened feeling turned to anger on how anyone could hurt a child like that. He turned back and stared into the eyes of the man in the catatonic state. His eyes were as cold as the ice he was buried behind. Curt's eyes filled with hatred as he punched into the face of the frozen man. He felt no pain in his hands as he proceeded to rapidly punch away like a boxer with his opponent on the ropes. Soon the ice cracked and Curt pummeled away until he felt the frozen flesh of this sickening man. He stopped, and lifted the man's head up, by pulling back on his hair. The man was heavy set. He had a rounded face with a cleft chin. His eyes were narrow and dark. Curt let go of the man's hair expecting his head to drop back down. "Do you like what I did? Would you like to join Babe Rafoe on finding young boys?" Laughter came from this man named Babe.

Curt was startled, but did not show it to Babe. "Go to Hell," as Curt realized how anticlimactic that sounded, since they were already there. Curt looked around to see if there was any way of freezing this scumbag back. Babe started using his breath to slowly melt the ice surrounding the rest of his body. Curt looked back at the entrance of the cave and noticed water flowing like a small stream from the heat from the steam outside. Running over, he removed his shoes and filled them with water. As he ran back he poured the slushy water over the face of Rafoe. Rafoe's mouth froze open. "Let's see how you like something shoved down your throat asshole." Curt poured the water down his throat and it instantly froze. Curt proceeded to pour more and more water over Rafoe, until he was completely frozen over again.

Curt realized he had to be careful and not let his temper get the best of him. He almost allowed the escape of a sick individual, whose only goal was to hurt young children. Looking at his frozen sneakers, he headed back out the cave and back into the steam. There he placed the sneakers back on his feet, as he composed his thoughts on how to proceed on his journey alone. "Things will get worse. I gotta stay prepared for anything," he thought to himself.

So he headed back towards the cave and noticed for the first time another entrance to the left. The entrance was much narrower but looked to head down deeper. Curt felt that was where he needed to go. Curt anticipated on seeing creatures with claws and tails protecting these entrances, but none were there. "Maybe they were all summoned to Heaven to protect their new treasure," he thought. Walking deeper into the coldest depths of Hell, he began to recognize famous faces. There he seen Napolean, Hitler, Stalin, and a new face of Bin Laden. He was surprised to see next to Bin Laden an open spot marked reserved for G.W. Bush.

He looked on the other side to see additional past presidents, senators, and congressmen of the United States, along with Presidents and dictators from other countries frozen. Certain spots were reserved for those who were still alive. Curt always knew how corrupt politics could be, but to be frozen for eternity in the depths of Hell, he didn't realize how corrupt the system was. He assumed that you really needed to sell your soul in order to become one of the world leaders.

It was then that he noticed a glow up ahead.

Chapter 20 Frozen In Time

The glow was so bright, yet easy to look at. In the frozen tundra of the inner depths of Hell, Curt could feel the warm glow ahead. As Curt walked closer and closer the warmth remained the same. Curt anticipated a burning bush once he was close enough. He knew he had reached God. He had so much to ask him, but the only question in his mind was "Why?"

Heaven and Hell was nothing like Curtis had pictured it. He always thought that when he died, all his emotions would no longer matter. He thought the answer to all his questions would be fulfilled. He thought he would be happy. Instead, he felt worse. He felt the pain of loss hundreds of times worse than he felt on earth. As he walked closer to the light, he began to feel remorse instead of happiness. The thought of turning back actually entered his mind, but quickly discounted that fact. If it wasn't God ahead, then what would he do? He left everything to faith. Except for his children on earth, every person that meant anything to him was here. Curt had no idea where they were or if that was it for them. Did they no longer exist in any way? Curt knew at this point it didn't matter. They weren't with him, except for in his heart. That brought solace to Curt.

Curt stopped and stared. At the end of his rocky frozen path, he finally reached his destination. Curt was in front of God. He looked like the image of God on the ceiling of the Sistine Chapel, but was frail like a very old George Burns. His index finger was outreached like Michelangelo's fresco. He was frozen deep into the side of Hell. Curt went up to the ice, first rubbing his hand to feel how smooth it was. Banging the ice with his hand, just made his fist ache. This time he couldn't penetrate through the ice with his fist. He looked around for a loose stone, but everything was frozen. He turned around to run down the path he came only to find his way out was frozen solid. Curt found himself trapped. Curt headed back toward God and again banged on the ice to no avail. He scratched at the ice, breathed on the ice, but was unable to make a mark.

Breathing heavily, Curt screamed at the top of his lungs as his voiced echoed off the walls. He kept screaming hoping the acoustics would crack the ice. But nothing happened. He stepped back to look at God, but was stopped by a frozen wall of ice that had formed behind him. Curt threw himself down to the ground. "So this is my destiny," as he talked to God through the ice. "I was that bad of a person, I ended up in the deepest depths of Hell. I had to watch my love ones die, again. The pain I lived wasn't enough. Now I must suffer my eternal life. So be it." Curt had no fight left as he dropped his head and noticed out of the corner of his eye a huge icicle forming to the right. He looked up at the ceiling and seen icicles above his head. He figured he would end up suffering through excruciating pain when one of the icicles would impale him, when it came crashing down. He remembered the image of the soul in the bloody river. "I certainly will suffer worse than he, because I am in the deepest depths of Hell."

Curt did not know how long he had sat there in self pity. He attempted to get up when he realized he was partially frozen in the ice. The back of his head, back, and legs were trapped in the ice. He shifted his body back and forth, releasing screams in fear, as he fought to free himself. He knew that his time was about to come, but he fought till the end. He was able to free his left shoulder and then his right. He rocked his legs until he freed them too. His torso soon followed. He pounded the ice around his head until it finally released him from his prison. He shot up quickly and began walking back and forth in his ever shrinking space that was no more than five feet long and only 3 feet wide, shrinking with every step. He felt like a caged animal at the zoo and wondered if they felt this same anxiety.

Still looking around for a way out in his ever shrinking cell, Curt finally came to the conclusion that there was no longer a sense of fighting his incarceration. With a sigh, Curt moved as close to his God, "I'm sorry I failed you. I failed you in life, and in this afterlife. As God as my witn...well you know what I mean, I really tried. I tried to be a good son, father, husband, worker, and especially a worshipper. I always tried, but rarely succeeded." Tears rolled down Curt's face. Curt wasn't ashamed or disappointed with himself, because he felt he did the best he could. "I just wasn't worthy." Curt looked up at God staring directly into his eyes. Curt's head was suddenly frozen, with his eyes wide open.

Curt's right leg was outstretch and frozen. His left leg he positioned up, bending at the knee. Soon they were frozen. The only movement Curt had was his left arm. With his eyes frozen open, staring at God, he pulled his left arm up, reaching his index finger out, like Adam in Michelangelo's fresco. Curt knew he failed his family as he failed in life. His final movement was to say in body language, that he tried. He did not succeed, but he knew he would succeed in this last ditch effort, that he Loved God, no matter what. With one final stretch of his finger, Curt found himself frozen for eternity, staring at the God he attempted to save.

Chapter 21 Imagine If

To Curt's surprise, he could still think. He rummaged through his thoughts, as they sporadically changed from childhood, to his children, his life, and his adventurous afterlife. The thoughts raced across his brain, not able to concentrate on any particular thought for any extended period of time. As these images of his life blinked by him, his ability to blink was gone and he was always brought back to the vision of God in front of him.

Curt imagined being able to stretch his finger closer to God, but knew he could not. So he focused all the energy to the tip of his finger, feeling the ice at the end of it. The ice didn't feel cold, but warm. The tip of his finger felt the warmth coming from God.

Curt focused on pressing his finger toward the warmth. His finger only moved in his head. However, the finger of God looked to move ever so slightly in the lower corner of Curt's vision. Was his imagination playing games with him? Curt wanted to believe this was happening. Again, from the corner of Curt's eye it looked as if God's finger moved closer to Curt's. Imagine if this was happening. Curt had a goal to attain. That was to reach the tip of God's finger. Curt concentrated harder and harder to move his finger toward God. As the hours went by and possibly days, Curt sensed the warmth becoming stronger.

Then it happened. Curt felt the rush of God's love enter him through their touching fingers. Curt experienced truly for the first time that God's love was real.

Curt's love of God acted like a jumper cable to God's love. Their energy traveled back and forth to each other. The warmth they created began to melt the ice around their bodies. The touch of their fingers soon turned into the grip of each other's hand. When their hands gripped, the energy exploded like a big bang, releasing them from their icy prison and left them face to face with each other.

Curt bowed his head down as he wrapped his arms around God. God's meek body became stronger as he grew into a more powerful vision that was now worthy of God's imagery. "Thank you, my son. You have released me from the depths of Hell."

The sound of God's voice humbled Curt. "My family," as he stuttered to find the right words, "they saved you. They led me here to you."

"Your belief in me and your love for me have given me hope for all of mankind." God looked at Curt like a caring parent. "You did well. I know you have questions, don't be afraid to ask."

Curt was stunned. He did not fear his God, but only felt pure love from God. "Wh…what happened? How did you end up here?"

"People had stopped believing on earth. As their quest for the truth grew, they figured out some of the truths about creation. As man's thirst for knowledge grew, man had accurately figured out how things had been created. Soon man had thought he was becoming God. So if man was becoming God, I no longer needed to exist. With the love of man disappearing, an overabundance of negative energy occurred. That made Satan stronger. He thrives on negative energy. As with Adam and Eve, I flawed with having Heaven and Hell. I allowed Satan to have all the negative energy, which made him a powerful foe. With his greed, he was no longer satisfied with Hell. Satan's greed was matched by many people on earth. He was able to trap me and place me here for all eternity."

Curt was dumbfounded. "How did he trap you?" Curt gazed in amazement of his conversation with God.

"He used your mother, without my knowledge."

"My mother helped Satan? Why, it does..."

God finished Curt's response and continued on, "...doesn't make sense. You are right, because your mother is a saint. Her belief never swayed. Her life was difficult. She had been born deaf, but man was able to help her hear. She was raped, beaten, and become pregnant. Every time she held your sister, who was a child of the rape, she felt love, never any bitterness. She suffered and survived cancer on more than one occasion, before succumbing to it. She lost her father in an auto accident, which for awhile affected both your parents. Your father became bitter as he had a closer relationship with your mother's father, than he had with his own father. They were best friends. Your mother was a strong willed woman who never flinched in her belief. There was only one thing that could occur that could ever question her faith. That would be a loss of a child. Not any child, but her young son. YOU." Curt was silent as he listened on, "Satan had given you the measles at birth, but the love and caring of your mother saved you. Then one day on the ice, I knew for the first time, your mother would question her belief in me. You felt a presence under the ice. You were not alone. I pushed you to safety."

"Thank you for saving me. So you needed to save me, so I could save you." Curt looked at God for reassurance."

"So you think this was all about you? This has never been about you." God's deep tone rose, scaring Curtis into silence. God dropped his tone and continued, "That split second under the ice was enough for Satan to make his move. He was able to trap me and bury me in Hell. Once that occurred, it was up to the love of man to save me. I give man the strength to fight off Satan, but it is man's will if he wishes to use this strength. Your mother had been through enough in her life. She lost the closest person to her in her father and her faith did not waiver. On earth, no matter how much you love your parent, the love of your children is a hundred thousand times greater. You are very aware of that," as God acknowledged Curt's love of his children. "Had I allowed you to drown, the questioning by your mother would have weakened me to the point Satan would have ruled Heaven for eternity. I knew I had to save you for your mother's soul. I need man to control his destiny. If a man walks in front of a car and is killed, so be it. If a plane crashes, so be it. If a child falls through the ice, so be it. I care and love all. If an early death brings a soul to me, I will love them, as I love you. The warmth and presence will send man onto the next level of their journey. You are only at the second level of a journey through enlightenment. Your mother is the key to enlightenment. I had to intervene, which gave Satan the upper hand. He was able to freeze me under the ice, when I pushed you to safety."

Curt felt nothing. He felt betrayed, because saving him really didn't matter? Then it hit him like a brick. "So man is basically on his own on earth? You only intervene when you have to?"

"Yes."

"How often do you intervene?"

"Rarely. Close to never."

"My mom was that important to you that you had to save me?"

"Yes, but you are very important to your mom."

Curt paused, finally understanding that God loved all, and all the pure Curt felt from his mother, was the same love he felt from God. Curt recognized the importance of God needing the pureness of his mother's soul. "I always realized what a great woman she is, I just didn't realize how great."

"It is time to make things right. Your mother would want it that way."

Curt was confused, "You say that like she no longer exists."

God acknowledged, "She does exist, as does your father, grandfather, and daughter. They have just moved on to the next level."

"So when do I see them?"

"You must attain the next level of the Heavens. You must understand there is a chain, between levels that must not be broken or we all become nothingness. This is our key to enlightenment. You have already seen them, it is the way."

"So be it." Curt walked next to God, feeling melancholy.

Chapter 22 Next Question

As the strength grew in God, he no longer looked like any man. He was larger than man. Curt could not help to feel like a pawn in a chess match. He felt used and isolated the more he thought about how his particular life didn't matter. "What is it my son? What is bothering you?" God asked in a fatherly manner.

"Nothing; I'm feeling selfish that's all."

"We are all one. When I criticized you for thinking it was not about all about you, please keep in mind, we needed you. Without you there is no more Heaven, no more levels, and no more enlightenment. You are an important piece of the chain, as are your parent, your grandparents, and especially your children.

Curt attempted to acknowledge what God was saying. "So you're saying, every life on earth has meaning?"

"Not, exactly." Man is the ultimate being on earth. How he learns to care for himself and others is learned. Man has grown from his ancestral beginning to where he is today. Man was no different from any other animal on earth. He has best adapted to his surroundings. Had man not adapted and had died off; I would have needed to re-create life on earth again. So you see, the ability to think needed to be developed. Once man was able to think, he began to question his existence. Man's ultimate quest has always been the growth of his spirituality. Many on earth have forgotten that. Without spiritual growth, there is no growth and man will cease to exist. Man is on the brink. Man must change his ways in order for his enlightenment to continue."

"What about Heaven and Hell? Why do they exist?"

"You need enlightenment. The pure love you feel today only becomes greater and greater. The knowledge you seek, becomes greater and greater. Heaven and Hell must exist in balance. If Satan becomes too powerful, he would seek all the energy. Without any positive energy, there would be no energy at all. There would be nothingness. As your God, I am able to provide the balance necessary to exist. I created Heaven and Hell to provide necessary balance.

Curt was overwhelmed what he was hearing. He stopped in his tracks and closed his eyes. He felt the pure love of God that he had only felt a few times before in his life. Curt knew his life on earth no longer mattered. The spiritual love was overwhelming. He began to cry, not out of sadness, but for the happiness he felt. He knew his mother, father, grandfather, and daughter were in a place of complete rapture. Curt knew that he had reached the next pinnacle of enlightenment.

Chapter 23 2nd Term

God and Curtis reached the point of all the world leaders who had been frozen into the depths of Hell.

"Why are they here?" Curt questioned. "Are politicians that corrupt?"

"On the contrary. Most politicians look to help all their people the best they possibly can. They make decisions which are not the most humanitarian. Sometimes they make mistakes. The truth is in their hearts. They follow what they believe to be the right thing to do. They were placed in Hell by Satan. They would have fought for the good of Heaven. That is why they are here."

"Shouldn't we release them? Shouldn't they help us, now?"

God looked over at each of the politicians. "They have also done things for their own gains. Let's leave them to think about their sins. We have a greater job to do now. Too many leaders will give us too many options. We don't have time for them to agree to disagree."

Curt looked over at the other wall, where Napolean, Hitler, Bin Laden, and a spot saved for George W. Bush. "I understand why they are here. But, why George Bush?"

"Again, he is a good man. He made mistakes. He took bad advice. His heart told him one thing and his advisors knowingly told him wrong. He knew his heart was right, but he followed bad, bad advice. I will place him here, until he acknowledges the error of his ways. He has already shown regret for some of his decisions. He is a good soul, who I need to grow spiritually." The two kept walking until they reached a point of chaos when they reached Pandora's Box. Curt made a motion to God to hide so he would not be seen, but God smiled. "My son, I hide from no one." God proceeded to walk toward Pandora's Box. "Who leads these men?"

"It is I. Do you wish to challenge me for the right to lead, these men?" Brutus stated, in a defiant voice. "Do you dare challenge me?"

"I challenge no one. I allow them to challenge me."

"Then I challenge you to death." Brutus pointed his club toward God. "Pick your weapon."

"Pick my weapon?" God laughed "I do not need a weapon. I have called you out to tell you to place these men back where they belong. If you do, I will make you a deal to allow you to rule Hades."

"I already rule Hades. Men...," as Brutus pointed his club at God and Curt, "DESTROY THEM!"

The dregs raised their swords, clubs, and chains and rushed to mutilate the souls of the two. Out of instinct Curt moved in front on God, as if he were protecting a child. A sword was swung at the head of Curt. He did not flinch. The sword came within a millimeter of his neck when it froze in place. The first few lines of the dregs were all frozen in place, as they were all turned to salt by God. An explosion sent the new salt pillars into millions of pieces of salt dust. The remaining dregs were turned to salt from the waist down, with just a small hand movement by God. The dregs screamed in fear, except one. Brutus looked down and back at God. "You are more powerful than I could have imagined. "Who are you?"

"I am your God. I decide the fate of men. I've decided yours. That is why you are here."

"So you allowed me to rules Hades for a short time. Now you turn half my body to salt. Why not just do away with me."

Many of the dregs between Brutus and God began to break the salt as an attempt to escape. Soon their half bodies lay on the ground. "You, that have destroyed yourselves, by breaking the salt, may have the remaining half of your bodies returned, by returning to Pandora's Box." A small light over the box came from a small opening too small for anyone to escape and seemed too small for anyone to enter. The first dreg closest to the box reached his arm over the light. The light broke down his body into a molecular level, showing the dregs his legs again. The molecular body was then sucked into Pandora's Box through the small opening. The light seemed to act like a vacuum, sucking the molecular dreg in. Once the others had seen this occur, they began to drag themselves towards Pandora's Box to regain their lower bodies, before being secluded back into the box. God looked over at Brutus "So you would like to control Hades, I can make this happen for you. First you must do me a favor and adhere to my plan." God walked over to Brutus, but had Curt stay back. He spoke for a few moments to Brutus, before changing his body back from the salt. Brutus looked down at his legs and then bowed to God. He then pointed at the men who he had requested be changed back. The men, who were again made whole, followed behind Brutus. The remaining men still frozen in salt, had their salt bodies smashed by Brutus and his men. The dismembered bodies were then tossed towards Pandora's Box and finished their journey by dragging themselves into the light. God walked back to Curt, "It is done."

Curt did not ask about the conversation between God and Brutus. Brutus acknowledged God leaving and pointed the way towards Heaven. Curt acknowledged his undeniable belief in God. He would not question God's intentions.

Soon God and Curtis reached the Gates of Hell, where the gate keeper was still moaning about the loss of coins. "Where are we headed?" Curt asked.

"I need to find my son, Jesus. I need to thank him for his prayers. Without his prayers, I am nothing."

Walking into the clouds where everything was again white, Curt turned to God and asked "Why not send your son back to earth? I think they would be more receptive than ever. People need to believe."

"I did send my son back to earth. His death ended up being a Twentieth Century crucifixion."

"Would I have known who he was?"

"He was born during your 2nd Great War. He was not born of a virgin, for this time I needed someone who would be born with sin. I wanted someone who would understand the wrongs of the world. He needed to live a sinful life in order to learn what peace was all about."

"World War II?" Curt was not sure what God meant when he said the 2nd Great war.

Annoyed, God corrected his statement so Curt would know the era. "Yes, he was born during World War II. The exact year was 1940. He was named after a great leader of his time, Winston Churchill. His father was a merchant seaman, who was gone for very long stints of time. His mother had a difficult time in raising him, so he was raised by his aunt. He was a rebellious fellow, a trouble maker really. His friend's parents did not like him, because he was disruptive. He was envious of the home life of his friends, because he didn't have much of one. He once stated that he wasn't raised by his parents, which made him see his parents were not Gods. He clearly left enough messages that he was the second coming of Christ, but people failed to realize this. He was very influential over his friends. He was artistic, and loved by millions, if not billions. He challenged the government, wrote and sang songs about peace. He even signed an album to the man, who killed him. He realized this man was distraught, so he even asked him if he could do anything else to help him. A few hours later Mark David Chapman, shot John Lennon."

Curt couldn't believe his ears. "John Lennon, really? That would make Yoko Ono, like, Mary Magdalene."

"Both are strong women in their own right. Both have been given bad raps. Mary Magdalene was not a whore, but came from a very wealthy family. She was denounced by the Catholic Church centuries after her death. Yoko was denounced by the media as the reason for breaking up the Beatles."

"But why did you choose John Lennon? Why not pick Paul McCartney? He had just as much influence? How was John Lennon named after Winston Churchill?"

"Do you have any more questions? Should I write them down? "God looked at Curt to see if he had any more questions. Embarrassed, Curt nodded no. "First, his full name is John Winston Lennon. He was an activist for peace. He was against war. His songs Imagine and Give Peace a Chance, to name a few, sent messages of hope to all. His life was filled with strife, but he found an inner peace with family and his belief in the spiritual world. Paul was very influential in the development of the Beatles music. He and John created a sound that influenced generations. Early on, John needed Paul. Paul was influential to John. They both needed to part ways to grow, individually and spiritually."

Curt listened to what God was saying and he was amazed. Curt just had one question left, "If John was the second coming of Christ, what did that make Paul?"

"Paul became a very rich and successful man."

"That's not what I meant; I meant what became of Paul spiritually in your eyes?"

"He became an apostle. He became an angel on earth. That is why after the Beatles broke up, I gave him Wings."

Chapter 24 Taylor Made

God and Curt walked and soon they seen crosses. "This is where I seen your son, last." Curt pointed to the rows and rows of crosses.

When they reached the crosses, Jesus was singing, <u>Imagine</u> to the masses. Jesus lifted his head up from looking at his guitar strings and seen his father. He handed the guitar to one of his disciples and hugged God like a small child hugging his father coming home from work. As they embraced, Jesus looked at Curt and smiled. His face changed from Jesus to John Lennon and back to Jesus. "I have Curt to thank for saving you."

"No, I have you for saving all of us," Curt lowered his head in respect to Jesus.

"How are the Heavens? Have you succeeded on retaining the Heavens?" God asked his son.

"I have stayed and prayed. The army that had gone to fight has met with much resistance. They are true warriors, but they need help."

"I have gotten the help they need. I will take our Heaven back." God reassured his son and his disciples. "How are you doing here?"

"Many more lost souls have found their way to us. We comfort them the best we can." Right at that moment, the sound of crying was coming from a little girl who was walking toward the masses. Jesus reached out to her as he picked her up and hugged her. She was about 9 years old. Her hair was long and dark and she had bloodstains on her chest. "Do not be afraid, I will help you. What is wrong?" Jesus then motioned his hand across her chest and the bleeding and scars from her wounds were healed.

The little girl turned her head on Jesus' shoulder, "You need to help my mom, she misses me and it hurts her."

"Can I help?" A boy around 7 asked Jesus as he came through the crowd. "My dad was the same way, I think I can help?" Jesus placed the little girl in the direction of the smaller boy. The boy had short blonde hair, with blue eyes, and was wearing a Yankees uniform. "When I came here, my dad cried for me every night. I lost my battle with Leukemia. I really, really tried to beat it, but I became too tired and could not fight the disease anymore. I would lie in bed, pretending to be asleep. My dad would come in and hold my hand and cry. He prayed for God to save me. I would sometimes roll over to the other side of the bed so he didn't see me cry. I would squeeze my dad's hand to try to reassure him. I wasn't afraid to die. I was just afraid of not seeing my dad anymore. Before I came here, they had a funeral for me. Lots of people got to see me in my favorite baseball uniform. They kept my baseball cap on so people would not see me without my hair. Look," as the little boy lifted his hat, "I got hair again. Anyway, on Christmas my father came to the cemetery where my body lay. He fell to his knees, his hands on top of the stone, his head laid on the stone. He was crying uncontrollably. That is when I broke through the shivering cold and shined warmth on his back. When he felt the warmth, I snuck down and hugged him. He felt me with him and cried harder at first, before he realized I was still with him. You can still be with your mom. Want me to show you?" The little girl nodded in acceptance. "What's your name?"

"Christina. My name is Christina Taylor Green."

"Neat. We have the same name. I am Taylor Evans." He smiled and took the little girl's hands and kneeled down with her. Christina stared at Taylor and then looked down. "Watch this." Taylor pushed away the white and an opening occurred. Curt looked curiously over the shoulder of Taylor. There came in view, a man staring at Taylor's picture on the wall. "That's my dad." The man touched the picture and began to cry. "I don't like to see my dad sad. Watch me make him happy." Sunlight appeared on the man's hand touching the picture. Right then a boy about 15 came into the room. "That's my brother, I sent him in there. He was all set to go downstairs to play video games, but I put a thought in his head to tell my dad good news."

"Hey dad, I'm the starting running back for Friday's game. Can you make it? Taylor's brother Dominic asked their dad.

"I wouldn't miss it for anything in the world. Congratulations, son. Your hard work paid off. I am very proud of you."

"My dad and brother are super close now. That's the way I like it." Taylor turned to Christina, "Do you wanna try?" Again, Christina nodded in acceptance. "Ok, here is the deal. You can't see them all the time. Sometimes they need their privacy. It's best when they are thinking of you."

Christina, with the help of Taylor, moved her hand over the white and suddenly her mom appeared. "That's my mom. She's at work."

"Let's have some fun. I'm gonna spill her coffee, but don't worry, I won't get it on her or ruin anything important." Taylor had the coffee cup spill by moving it closer to Christina's mom's arm. She quickly grabbed some tissues by her computer and wiped up the coffee. As she turned to grab a few more tissues, the reflection of light from the clear coffee cup shined on Christina's picture on her desk. Her mom forgot about her coffee mess for a moment and picked up her daughter's picture and embraced it. "Now, go down and hug her."

Christina, shot down like light and held her mother. "I love you, mom. I'll be okay and so will you."

"Pretty neat, huh?" Taylor was proud of what he showed her.

"I think she heard me, talk to her."

"Kinda, sorta. You're new so I had to help you out." Taylor responded. "Just finish watching." Christina's mom envisioned hearing her daughter. She then realized she heard the woman in the next cubicle talking to her mother, about the loss of her father. Turning back to stare at the picture, a glimmer seemed to come from Christina's eye, almost like a wink. Her mom stared at the picture, kissed it and put it back down, before completing her clean up of the coffee. "Now, you can pretty much do this when you want." The white reappeared where Christina seen her mom, "You can do this with anyone you wish. Just don't do it too much or it won't be special anymore."

Curt bent down to attempt seeing his children. He was not able to see them. "Taylor, can you help me out here? Can you show me how to see my kids?"

Taylor looked at Curt, then at God in puzzlement. "That only works for kids." Taylor looked back at Curt.

Curt turned his attention to God, "I miss my kids too. Why can't I see them?"

God in his wisdom stated, "Parents who lose a child, need to know they are okay. Kids are stronger and are able to adapt to a loss of a parent. Some day you will be back together with them. In Heaven, time doesn't matter. What can seem like an eternity on earth is only a mere moment in Heaven. You still have your mortal feet. Now use them to follow me to the Pearly Gates to take back what is rightfully ours."

As God, Jesus, and Curt walked, the massed followed.

Chapter 25 The New Beginning

The mass of people made it to the Gates of Heaven and they noticed mythical looking creatures losing their fight to the army led by Joe. Joe had done what he said he would do; he had taken back part of Heaven. "There is still work to do." Joe gave an updated report to the three souls in front of him. "I will need your help to complete our mission." Joe bowed to the presence of God. "Satan is too strong for the souls of mortals to overcome. I ask that you help us complete our journey.

"You are a very brave man." God responded. "More men should be like you."

The ground began to shake in a violent quake, sending the masses everywhere. God lifted his arms and silenced the ground below. The skies darkened as did the white around them, as a showdown was coming. A piercing scream came from the Heavens. A voice that sounded like it was underwater, but could be heard clearly; spoke to the people just outside the Pearly Gates. "You have played your cards and will lose, as I am the greatest force in the Kingdom." Satan had addressed the masses, with his cat like eye contact directly at God. His skin was red and burnt with pus and clear fluids making his skin shine. His chin pointed like an arrow, while his yellow teeth were sharpened like a piranha. Satan pointed his sharpened fingernails at God and leashed a fireball directly at him. "I will rule for eternity." Satan laughed.

Instinctively, Curtis dove in front of God. The fireball exploded in front of Curt, but it did not leave a mark on him. He looked around to see if everyone was okay when he noticed a burnt flesh moving in front of him. Joe had jumped in front of Curtis taking the hit of the fireball. He tried to raise his charred body up, but collapsed as his spirit was no more. Satan had destroyed the honorable Joe.

"Your most honorable fighter is no more. Do you wish to succumb to my powers or be destroyed by them?" Satan questioned God.

God moved Curtis from the path that destroyed Joe and proceeded to bring himself in front of Satan. "For many years, you have taken the upper hand. I had allowed you to be too strong. I thought man would come to my defense. You have tricked them by giving them greed. Now I need to take command and weaken you. You will no longer lead but will live in solitary confinement in a new depth of burning that only you will endure."

"How do you plan to do this? With him? Satan pointed at Curt and laughed. "I hold the upper hand of power that I control with greed. This new confinement you have made for me will only be inhabited by you."

"We shall see. However, I fight fire with fire. In your case I will fight greed with greed." God motioned his hand to show an army led by Brutus ready to attack Satan. "I have offered him the opportunity to rule Hell. You will be nothing. By changing your army from Hell, I have changed the negative energy and replaced it with positive energy. I now hold the upper hand."

Satan at first held his ground when Brutus' army attacked. The first few lines of troops were destroyed by Satan. However, one by one they were able to attack Satan, bringing him to his knees. God pointed to the side where Curt seen Pandora's Box. This time black smoke emulated from the corner. Curt picked up the box and walked toward Satan. Satan hissed, but Curt wasn't afraid. "Goodbye, Satan." Curt placed the box on the chest of Satan.

Satan's skin began to melt and form a funnel above Pandora's Box. The box itself melted through the chest of Satan to ground below him. The troops of Satan were sucked in Pandora's Box first, being crushed like a man's body in the depths of the oceans. The troops were followed by the mythical creatures having the same fate. Satan knew he was defeated and lashed out one final time toward God by raising his head and sending all his negative powers to the almighty. God in turn did the same. An explosion of the energies caused a blast ten million times stronger than any nuclear explosion on earth. The white light was brighter than any light Curtis had ever envisioned. All the darkness in the Heavens was gone. Everything again was white.

The army of Brutus was gone. All of Satan's creatures and army were gone. Satan was gone. The massed bowed to God. "Satan is no more of a threat. Brutus now reigns in Hell. Brutus realizes the power and will abide by my wishes. God's energy will rule for eternity."

Chapter 26 Going, Going, Gone

Curt was thrilled at seeing the victory of Good over evil. Good over evil. The words themselves had special meaning. Good is God with an extra o, for the overwhelming victory of the devil. Evil is the devil without the d, for defeated. Curt's excitement peaked when he looked into Heaven's door and seen his family looking out at him. Joe, his grandfather, father, mother, and his daughter Angel all smiled, as the women threw him kisses and the men pumped their fist in the air. Curt's dad followed the pump in the air by covering his heart and tapping his chest, showing Curt his acknowledgement of his son's accomplishments. Curt stepped toward them, but was stopped by God. "No, Curt it is not your time to cross over to the other side."

"Not my time? My family is waiting for me." Curt pointed to his family who were now all hugging each other.

"I told you that you had your mortal feet. You need to go back."

Curt was torn by the knowledge that he would be back with his children, but still wished to be with his family, especially Angel. "What about my family?"

"They have escalated to the next level of the Heavens. They will wait for you when it's your time. Right now, you will go back to earth. You need to tell people your story. You need to tell them to believe in me again. I will send a message to them on the night of the Leonids shower. The world will all see the message. You need to tell them its coming."

"Can I hug them; can I hug Angel one more time?"

God motioned Curt to turn around and there were all his family members waiting to say goodbye. Curt hugged each one. "Grandpa thank you for being so strong, when I was weak."

"Stay strong and stay honorable. We will be together again." Sr. hugged his grandson.

"Dad you saved my life. I wish I had more time to spend with you."

"We will have an eternity." Jr. kissed his son on the cheek and hugged him.

"Mom, I barely seen you. I miss you so much."

"Honey, I need to tell your daughter about my son. I need time to spend with her. Don't worry, I will take good care of her." Curt kissed his mom and hugged her, holding her hand as tears began to roll down his cheeks. June pulled back to look at her son and handed his hand over to Angel.

Curt was crying, not out of sadness but happiness that he finally met his daughter. He only wished he had more time. He knew they would be together again. "I don't know what to say, other than I love you. I love you so much." Curt's eyes were blurred by the tears streaming out. "I wish I could bring you back with me, to meet your brother and sister. I want the four of us to be together. I want to always be a part of your life. I've been without you too long. I love you, I love you, I love you my Angel."

"I love you too. I am glad that we were finally together. I can tell you one thing. You just didn't father me, but the pure love that you have given me allows me to know that you're my dad." Angel and Curt hugged, with Curt kissing her hundreds of times all over her face. With one last hug, Angel took the hand of June and they joined the rest of the family.

"June! June! June is that you!" A voice coming from the next level of heaven was heard.

June turned and seen her father. "DAD," as the excitement was uncontrollable. She turned back to Curt, "that's your other grandfather. My Dad."

"Go mom, he has been waiting a long time to see you." Curt smiled as June ran to her dad bringing Angel with her. They hugged as they were joined by the others. They looked one last time to Curt and waved before walking away into the white.

"I LOVE YOU ALL!" Curt yelled as he stepped toward their direction. As he stepped down, the white ground disappeared and Curt was falling again. This time, everything went black.

Chapter 27 Don't Wake Daddy

Sitting by the bedside, Crystal held her dad's hand, laying her head on his shoulder. Her brother, Colin sat on a reclining chair bored, but not complaining about it. Their mother, Christy looked at her watch, before looking at Colin and smiling. Christy was leaning on the window sill of the 15th floor of Mercy Hospital. She thought about how much Curt would have hated being at this hospital.

Curt hated this hospital. He referred to it as Merciless hospital, because of how he was treated, or not treated for his kidney stones. Curt had entered the emergency room in severe pain. He was told they would take him in a few minutes. 5 hours later he was still waiting for someone to help him. Curt was dry heaving, in between his walks across the room. When he asked for the 15th time how much longer, the nurse shut the door on him, locking the room between her and the rest of the emergency room. Other patients even mentioned to the nursing staff, that this guy looked like he was ready to have a heart attack from the pain he was suffering. Curt's lungs started to fill with fluid, as his body could not handle much more pain. The security guard finally walked over to Curt and handed him a small plastic bowl. "If you feel like you're going to be sick, try to make it to the bathroom."

Curt couldn't believe what he had just heard. After finishing his dry heaves he grabbed the plastic container from the security guards hand and threw it towards the nurse's station and stated "If I could puke, piss and shit all over this Goddamn floor right now, I would. What the hell is wrong with you people? You're killing me!"

"There is no room, you'll have to wait." The security guard walked back behind his station.

"Screw this." Curt walked over to the guard and ripped off the plastic medical bracelet on his wrist. When the bracelet snapped, Curt's momentum from ripping off the bracelet hurled his hand upward, striking the security guard in the face. "I better not see a bill, fuck this place." Curt walked out the door to his waiting ride Christy who had just walked in. Curt thought for sure he was about to be arrested for hitting the guard. Unintentional, but still he hit the guy in the face. The guard just stood there shocked, either afraid of escalating the situation, or realizing Curt's frustration over the situation.

Christy drove Curt to an emergency clinic, where they immediately eased Curt's pain. Then Curt was transported back to Merciless hospital where he needed emergency surgery to remove the stone. Curt was aggravated he had to go back to Mercy, but he had no choice. When he paid his co-pays to the hospital he made the checks out to "Merciless Hospital."

Curt always said he would drop dead before he would step back into that hospital. Now here he was for the last 27 days. The hospital was making arrangements to move him to a nursing home the next day. "Okay Crystal, you still have homework. Let's go, honey." Christy said as she motioned to Colin to put on his jacket.

"Five minutes, please?" Crystal begged as her voice choked up. She did not want to leave her father's side.

"Honey, the hospital is going to move daddy tomorrow to a place where you can spend more time with him. You have to finish your homework. You know your dad would be disappointed with you if he knew your homework wasn't done."

"Just five minutes, I won't ask to stay any longer."

"Okay; five minutes. Colin and I will be in the hallway. Say goodbye to your dad Colin." Colin walked up to his dad, pushing his sister out of the way. "Knock it off you two." Christy warned them both.

"Bye, daddy." Colin kissed his dad on the cheek. Tears formed in his eyes. "I miss you daddy. Please come back." Colin reached over and hugged his dad's head.

Christy pulled him back and hugged her son before telling Crystal, "We will be in the hallway, not too long, okay?"

Crystal nodded as Christy and Colin walked out of the room. Christy said goodbye to the people on the other side of the curtain, who were sharing the room with them. Colin walked with his head down and flipped his arm up and down quickly as if to say a quick goodbye to the strangers he had been acquainted with for the past week.

Whispering under her breath, so the people on the other side of the curtain couldn't hear here, Crystal told her dad, "Don't worry, I'm doing good in school. I promise I won't let you down. I love you, daddy." Crystal gave her dad a bunch of kisses on his forehead, because the whiskers on his cheeks pricked her when she kissed him. Crystal looked at him for a few more minutes. She heard her mom say to Colin, that she would go back and get her in a minute. "Bye daddy, I gotta go."

Mumbling out, "Tell your mom, 5 more minutes," as Curt spoke for the first time in almost a month.

Shocked, Crystal screamed, first out of fear, then out of excitement. Christy ran in as Colin stood by the door shaking in fear. A nurse heard the scream and seen Colin panicking and headed quickly toward the room, reassuring Colin as she walked in. To Christy, Crystal, the nurse, and the people who were on the other side of the curtain, who had moved in to help the little girl, were all delighted to see Curt's eyes open. "Welcome back, your kids have been waiting for you," the nurse was startled at Curt's sudden alertness.

Curt was oblivious to the other's around, as he stared at his daughter. "What a beautiful sight. How is my princess?" Curt reached his arms out to her as she hugged him. "Where's your brother?"

"Colin, come see dad!"

Colin was still confused as his mother reassured him it was okay, as she dragged him into the room, towards his dad. Colin's eyes lit up, when he seen his dad hugging Crystal. "DAD!" Colin jumped on the bed and began hugging his dad. The nurse and his mom were concerned and tried to get Colin off the bed.

"Hey buddy, how are you?" Curt was so happy to be with his kids.

"Okay guys, give your dad some room, he's been through a lot," the nurse said sternly as she wanted to insure their enthusiasm would not cause any damage to their dad's fragile body.

"They're fine. Believe me, they are fine." Curt hugged his children. "How long have I been here?"

"Almost a month, we were ready to ship you out tomorrow." The nurse attempted to take his blood pressure, after getting the children to back away from their dad. "You're so alert, like you just woke up. It's like a miracle."

"It is a miracle. Wow. A month, it felt like minutes. Wow. God was right, time is different."

"What? Umm, what do you mean God was right?" Christy asked Curt, knowing he wasn't the most religious guy in the world. Everyone else looked at him strangely.

"Hey, Christy; thanks for bringing the kids up to visit. Yeah, I was with God. I know; I know what everyone is thinking. I'm not crazy, I didn't imagine it, and I can tell you, I was with God. Not only God, but Jesus, my parents, my grandfather, and my oldest child."

"Your oldest child?" Christy's head snapped back as she attempted to comprehend what Curt was talking about.

"I talked to you about Denise and her pregnancy she gave up. Well, I finally met my daughter." Curt looked at his kids, "Your older sister is awesome."

"I think you need your rest," the nurse chimed in.

"I'm fine. I'm telling you this wasn't a dream. It started with my Uncle Paul...."

Christy interrupted, "Curt, I came with the kids and told you while you were in your coma, your Uncle died."

"That actually makes sense. Not that I heard you in my coma, but that Uncle Paul died. I had seen him. He was the first person I met. Did he die the same day as my accident?"

"Actually, yes," Christy was shocked as everyone in the room suddenly became more intrigued."

"Listen," Curt adjusted himself in bed, while having Crystal climb in next to him as Colin was already comfortable on the other side, "I have seen Heaven and I have seen Hell. I have to tell you what happened to me." The people visiting the other patient in the bed next to them offered to give Curt's family their privacy, but felt a little obligated to listen, when Curt told them, "It's a great journey. I think you would be interested on listening to my story if you wish." They nodded in approval. "I'll start when I met my Uncle Paul..." Curt talked about his Uncle, meeting of demons, walking to Heaven, to meeting Angel and God. When Curt mentioned Angel a warm breeze was felt by all in the room on the 15th floor. They all thought it, but nobody mentioned it, until they felt it a second time. "I just felt my daughter Angel hugging us."

At this point, everyone's belief of a dream in a coma, to understanding that this actually happened to Curt, changed the way they viewed Curt. They were in awe of him. "May I touch your arm?" The older woman visiting asked Curt. "I want to touch someone who was touched by God."

Curt reached over and held the hand of the woman. "I am just like you. I am no one special. God asked me to bring back a message. That's what I need to do."

"What's the message?" The woman asked.

"God wants us to know that he exists. We all need to know this. He told me he would be sending a message to earth for all who wish to see, will see. God told me he would send the message in the sky on a night in November."

"Next month? You need to get your message, out. My daughter is a reporter. I think she would like to do a story about your journey." The woman announced.

"I can tell you one thing about my ex-husband," as Christy addressed the woman, "in all my years of knowing him, he was never one to go to church, but for some reason, you knew he believed. " Christy turned her attention to Curt, "He was never one to lie. I think having your daughter come in is a pretty good idea." Christy leaned over Curt and kissed him on his cheek, "It's good to have you back."

The nurse, who had stayed to listen to Curt, looked at the clock, seeing it was well past visiting hours, "Any interview will have to wait until tomorrow. I hate to say it, but I have to kick you all out, visiting time is over, and I am so behind on rounds. Thank God, I mean, good thing it slow up here tonight." Before she walked out of the room, she turned to Curt, "Mr. Schmidt, I look forward to hearing more of your message and seeing a message from God. This world really needs it. Welcome back." She turned and left the room.

The children hugged their father, before leaving for the night, with a skip in their step that they had missed for a month. Christy had already decided to let the kids stay home from school tomorrow, so they could spend the day with their dad.

Chapter 28 15 Minutes

Curt's recovery was considered by the doctors as amazing. Other than some stiffness from not moving, he seemed in perfect health. He did have a reminder of the scar he left himself on the back of his head. However, he had no medical issues from his coma. A television reporter, who worked for channel two, stopped by the hospital the next day to interview Curt. He declined, stating he just wanted to go home.

"You need to get your story out," Lorissa Burnett told Curt. Lorissa had worked at the station for about 3 years and had recently been promoted to weekend anchor. She was much taller in person , than Curt expected when she showed up at his hospital room with a cameraman. "From what my mother told me, your story is pretty amazing." Lorissa smiled showing her pearly whites and incredibly deep dimples. Her blue eyes were captivating and Curt could not help but stare at this beautiful woman in front of him.

"Right now, I just want to go home. I want to get cleaned and showered. I feel a little uncomfortable having a camera on me, when I'm in a gown with no underwear on." Curt lifted the covers as to look for his missing undergarment. "I promise to call you; I look forward to going home again."

"Here is my card. That is my direct cell number. You can call me anytime." Lorissa smiled and pointed her cameraman toward the door. "Looks like my Uncle, was sent home this morning," as she viewed the bed all made up and empty.

"Your mom picked him up; they both seem like great people."

"That's funny, because that's what my mom said about you."

"She doesn't know me very well, but I'll take the compliment." Curt smiled as he was being flirtatious with a woman 20 years his junior.

"Well, you should. Now remember to call me. I look forward to it." Lorissa headed out of the room saying something to her cameraman, that Curt couldn't hear.

"Did you see how that old guy was flirting with me? Gross!" Curt thought to himself what Lorissa was saying to her cameraman. "She wouldn't even give me the time of day. Didn't even know I existed," as an old Jon Lovitz bit ran through his head.

"Daddy" Crystal and Colin rushed into the room.

"You guys here to take me home? Who is driving? Crystal?" Curt hugged his kids as his ex-wife walked in to drive him home.

"So, are you ready to leave this hospital?" Christy asked, knowing full well what his response would be.

The ride home for Curt opened his eyes and ears to the sights and sounds around him. The birds seemed happier, the sound of his children laughing in the backseat, even the older buildings seem to have vibrancy to them.

Christy pulled into the driveway and Curt pressed the garage door opener he had given her and viewed the garage like a scene in a movie. Curt noticed a spot of blood on the workbench. Christy missed cleaning up. He stood outside the garage, staring inside. His kids ran into the house and turned on the television. Christy brushed his shoulder with her gloved hand and proceeded in the house through the garage. "What now?" Curt mumbled under his breath. "I'll give myself a couple days, get my resume together and find myself a job," his thoughts continued. "I just wanted a nice home, with a nice family, working a good job..."

"Daddy you're on TV." Crystal ran to the door.

Christy was laughing, "You better see this."

Curt walked into the house and Lorissa Burnett was talking to her mother. "This man was with God," Mrs. Burnett announced. "He told us about his unbelievable; let me rephrase that, his truly believable journey with God. I believe this man walked with our Lord and Savior."

"I guess the word is out. However, it sounds awfully embarrassing hearing it from someone else." Curt admitted to his family.

Lorissa wrapped up the interview by saying "Curtis Schmidt's recovery from a deep coma, to being nearly 100% healthy is a medical miracle. The light shining in when he talked about his lost daughter was too coincidental not to be a miracle. Curtis Schmidt has walked with God, giving hope to all who believe. Back, to you Chet."

The anchor commented, "That is wonderful Lorissa. But not as wonderful of another miracle of the missing Utah boy, being found alive...get this, by his own dog. Details, after this." Chet picked up the sheets of paper in front of him and tapped them on the table, before breaking for a commercial.

"How was I on the TV?"

"She asked you to tell your story. You said you wanted to go home and that you felt uncomfortable. She said something like you are a humble man and you responded, "I'll take that as a compliment. She said she had just one more question, how is heaven? Do you want to go back? Your response was that you looked forward to going home again. I can't believe you let them interview you the way you looked. Nice hospital gown." Christy laughed, "You could've at least shaved."

"I didn't know I was being taped. I'll tell you what, that was some very good use of editing. I'll give her credit for that. She probably felt, I wouldn't call her," Curt was interrupted by the phone ringing.

"Hello?" Christy answered the phone, "Who is this? You're from where? Hang on; I'll let you talk to him. You aren't going to believe this," as Christy placed her hand over the phone, "but some producer from the VIEW, wants to interview you on television."

Curt took the phone and talked, not believing the caller at first. The phone kept clicking that another call was incoming. By the time Curt agreed to do the interview, he had 4 other messages, requesting the same. Piers Morgan Tonight, Entertainment Tonight, The Joy Behar Show, and a show called Faith and Culture on EWTN network. The phone kept ringing and Curt turned down the ringer, allowing all the calls to go to voicemail. Soon people started showing up at the front door. First neighbors, then friends, followed by people he had never met. For the safety of his children he had Christy take the kids back to her home, upsetting his children. "This will just be for a little while, I promise," as he kissed both kids goodbye as a line of traffic was already to form in front of his house. Curt told his story to all those who came to listen. He agreed to talk to the VIEW and agreed to the morning talk show circuit, starting with the Today Show and ending on Good Morning America. He also agreed to be on Piers Morgan, but declined Dr. Phil, all religious shows, all entertainment shows, and all politically driven shows. Curt wanted the message to be just that, a message from God. He did not want politics or religion to skew what he had seen. Curt was Protestant, but knew that didn't matter. This wasn't about being Protestant, Lutheran, Catholic, Jewish, Muslim, Buddhist, or any other religion. He also didn't want to turn the message into a three ring circus.

The morning shows handled him with kid gloves allowing him to briefly tell his story, with some hinting he should write a book about his experience. He had a very powerful conversation with Piers Morgan, who clearly was a firm believer in God. During their conversation Piers asked, "Not too long ago, I had Penn Jillette on regarding his book God, No. I told him that he angered me. His book title, God, No, was a deliberate provocative statement. He meant to annoy those who believe in God. He responded that the only way we can share the universe and share humanity is talking strongly in what we believe in. Here's a clip:" The clip showed Piers and Penn expressing their opinions on whether a spiritual being existed. They discussed whether or not the universe is even comprehensible. Penn talked about why we can't be humble to the fact that we don't know. Piers questioned Penn on where we go when we die. Penn questioned what the difference was by saying, some things are beyond our comprehension and I don't know. "What do you think of his response?"

Curt leaned forward toward Pier and gave an answer which surprised Piers. "I would say he is right."

"He's right? How can that be? Your reason for being on the show is you walked with God and now you're saying an atheist is right?"

"An atheist wants proof. Penn is looking for proof of the existence of God. Why else would he write the book? He wants to believe in God, but he has no proof. If proof of God is given to Mr. Jillette, then he would surely come around and believe. He isn't an atheist, he is more of a belatheist."

"A belatheist?"

"That is what I call an atheist who wants to believe in God. A belatheist. Someone, who will eventually come around to the fact that God exists. To be honest, I am not very much different than Penn Jillette. I am not a religious man. I do not believe one religion is better than another. I believe they are all tools to a greater goal of reaching a spiritual awareness."

"You have provided proof of God's existence. Shouldn't that be enough?"

"What proof? My word is not enough. He needs to see the signs all around for himself. Believe me, there is no such thing as a true atheist. The reason I say this, is if he is a true atheist, why is he looking for signs to begin with?

Just because he hasn't found any signs or may have disregarded many as coincidence or luck doesn't mean he hasn't seen them. He is just not accepting of them. The fact that he is looking for these signs, isn't he looking for God? So whether he wants to admit this or not, he wants to believe. He is looking for answers. Penn mentioned how you felt about the year 1890, because you weren't born yet. I would have loved if you asked him how he felt about Jules Verne. What about Gene Roddenberry or even George Orwell? Weren't all these men visionaries? Haven't what they wrote go from fiction to nonfiction? Who is to say people like Rembrandt or Da Vinci haven't had the same visions in their paintings? I don't think it's his ego that is preventing him from seeing the truth. He is a very outspoken man who just likes to deal with facts. I just think Mr. Jillette is just missing the signals. The fact that he is looking for God, deep down he knows he exists. Maybe this scares him, because he feels God hasn't touched him or maybe things he has seen in his life weren't warrant an existence in God. I know I've been there. One day he will open his eyes differently and he will start to see the signs all around. Then he will be at peace with God.

Curt wrapped up his interview with Piers Morgan. His next planned and final interview was the VIEW. Curt felt all the interviews had gone well. Piers Morgan asked some challenging questions, but nothing Curt couldn't handle.

However, he was about to be blasted by the women of the VIEW.

Chapter 29 Seriously, That's Your View

Curt was introduced onto the stage in front of a live studio audience for the first time. He was feeling nervous speaking in front of this many people. When he was in the other studios, he was able to concentrate on the interviewer. Now he was being seated with 2 interviewers on one side and 2 on the other, with the studio audience straight ahead. Sitting to the left of Curt was Whoopi and Joy and on his right, Sherry and Elizabeth. Barbara was not there as she was working on an upcoming special, to be aired later on.

The interview started with a typical welcome and some questions from Elizabeth and Sherry. Whoopi joked about seeing some of her family in heaven again, because she thought she finally got away from them. The studio audience laughed and Curt smiled as he was about to give his response, when Joy jumped in matter of fact "C'mon, people really? There is no Heaven. There is no Heaven, no Hell, no nothing, you die, and that's it."

"Aw, c'mon" Elizabeth chimed in.

"Wait a minute, wait a minute," Whoopi jumped in "don't tell me I played a nun for nothing. Let's hear her reason." Whoopi turned to the audience who were laughing at her nun joke. "Hang on, hang on, let's hear what Joy has to say."

"Honestly, I think the whole thing is fabricated. I think this is an agenda about abortion. The mother was ripped apart. It sickens me that you would hide behind a so called God to get your agenda out."

Elizabeth became very upset with Joy, but the majority of the studio audience became intrigued that they may have been duped by Curt. Plus the stage hand controlling the audience reactions was making an ooohh sound with his lips, which many of the audience followed. "Okay, calm down everybody, calm down," as Whoopi stood up motioning her hands up and down to calm the audience. "Joy brings up a good point, but I'd like to hear Mr. Schmidt's response. What do you think about what Joy said?"

"What I think is that this isn't about me. This isn't about any agenda I have. I am telling you what happened. I am telling you the only agenda I have is to get out God's message."

"You're telling us what happened. You imagined this in your coma." Joy blasted Curt.

"I can't make you believe. I can only tell you the facts of my journey. I am not asking for donations, I am not asking to spread any agenda, I am only trying to help."

"Help?" Joy laughed. "By telling some poor girl out there who was raped, that God doesn't want her to get an abortion? Yeah, you're not pushing any agenda."

"This isn't about abortions. I'm telling you what happened." Curt's face began to turn red and his voice deepened out of frustration. "This is about God needing us to believe. He is not asking us to change our lives. He is asking us to do the right thing. Just because the Supreme Court has allowed abortions to be legal, doesn't make it right in the eyes of God". Then Curt said something that lost him to the audience. He gave a personal opinion on abortion. "I should have a daughter here today with me, but the convenience of an abortion had taken her away. At least I know she is with God."

"Sounds like you have issues. You sound like you're, I don't know, schizophrenic or something. I think you're attempting to take away women's rights." Joy pumped her fist in the air and began chanting "Women's rights, Women's rights," with the audience joining with her.

"Whoopi jumped in "Okay people, okay, that's enough." A smile was on her face. "We will just have to wait to find out if Mr. Schmidt is right. November 17 is the date God is sending a message, is that the right date?" Curt acknowledged without commenting further, as the statement from Whoopi sounded half mockingly. "Remember God, I played a nun for you. When we come back from break we will be joined by Mariah Carey, who will sing her hit song of her new CD. Stick around, we will be right back."

Curt sat dumbfounded as a producer ran onto stage and escorted him off. "That went well." Joy laughed as she adjusted the strap on her bra as she walked back to the desk at the other end of the stage where she grabbed her seat. She yelled over to Curt "Next time you won't turn down an interview on my show." A hairstylist and makeup artist rushed over to her fixing her up for the next segment. "I'll just put him on the spot here," talking to the makeup artist. "It drives me crazy, some of the people we are forced to interview."

Curt felt his message from God was lost. He felt awful he let down God.

Chapter 30 Extra, Extra, Read All About It

Curt walked through the parking lot toward Wegman's grocery store he knew what a professional athlete must constantly feel. Staring straight ahead as he walked, he could feel eyes piercing him like daggers. He heard the heads of people snap around locking him in sight as if they were human weaponry. All he could do was keep walking straight and not make eye contact. He entered the vestibule, walking by the rows of shopping carts and grabbed a small basket to the left of the lottery machines. He turned to the left and headed toward the deli counter, when he notice the front page of the local news. "A skewed View," was the heading. A sub title read "Local man's odd perspective draws much criticism across country."

Under the caption was a picture of Curt on the View. His arms were raised as he was explaining what he had witnessed. He looked like Jesus at the last supper, with half the panel to one side and the other half to the opposite side. "Wow, it must have been really a slow news day, to make front page news," he thought to himself as he picked up the paper. "I guess any and all publicity really is better than none. I hope that people, who see this, will become believers and not more skeptical," as his thoughts continued.

Curt picked up the paper and was reading the opening paragraph, when he was startled by a voice that came up from the side of him. "Wow, that's you in the paper" a heavy set man in his forties, with a beard and glasses stated the obvious. "I hate to bother you, what you said on television yesterday, is it really true?" The man's voice was deep from the nervousness of approaching Curt.

Curt turned and looked directly at a man, who was staring squarely at him. Curt could see the man had heaviness in his eyes that went deep in the soul of his being, which was heavier than his actual overweight body. The man was looking for more than a simple yes response. "Everything I said is true. All I was looking to do was tell what happened to me. I guess I said too much and things were taken out of context. Now if you excuse me, I need to pick up a few things and head home."

Curt placed the paper back on the rack and headed back toward the deli counter. He stopped and took a number to lock his place in turn. He backed up and away from the counter until his turn. He had number 26. "14, number 14," Curt knew he would be waiting a few minutes for his turn.

"Excuse me, I'm sorry to bother you again, my name is Gary by the way," the heavy set man coming up to Curt to continue their short lived conversation, "Can you just answer one question for me? Please?" Curt noticed people forming a small semicircle, leaving him and Gary in what seemed like an ultimate fighter showdown. "My son died of Leukemia" Gary's voice began cracking, "I gotta know if in heaven he doesn't have any more pain," as a tear uncontrollably rolled down his cheek.

"Listen, don't worry. I'm sure your s..." Curt stopped in mid sentence realizing who Gary was. "My God, it's you. I've seen you in heaven. I mean, I seen you when I was in Heaven. I was looking down at you, with Taylor. You're Taylor's dad!"

Gary froze. For a split second, he stopped breathing. Shock had overwhelmed his body, before his shoulders slumped, his head dropped, bringing his hands up over his face, before he broke down crying. Curt hugged him and whispered "It's okay, your son is okay."

Gary quickly gathered himself, wiping his eyes with the palm of his hand. "You're sure it was him, my Taylor, my baby boy, are you sure?"

"He was wearing a baseball uniform. Not just any uniform, but a Yankees uniform. He talked about how you used to take him to different ball parks. He enjoyed going to Yankee stadium. He mentioned how you tried to catch a foul ball on the first base line, but it hit your hands and if fell to the lower deck. He knows that you didn't catch the ball, that you bought him the one you handed him. It was his favorite gift."

"I had it in my hands." Gary cusped his hands while reenacting his motions. "Somehow, it bounced out and fell. I yelled down to the lower deck and yelled, can I have the ball back for my kid? I'll be right down. I told Taylor to stay right in his seat and I would be right back with the ball. I ran to the souvenir stand and bought a ball. I then took it out of the box and scuffed the ball on the cement. I went back to the seat and told him the nice man gave me the ball back for him. He couldn't believe his eyes, he was so excited." Gary's tear had turned into a smile before he began to cry again. "We buried him in a Yankees uniform. God, I miss him."

"Don't worry, he can see you. Not all the time, but he can see you."

"Bullshit" a voice came from the crowd. "What the hell are you doing to this guy? Can't you see he's hurting enough?" A man with short dark curly hair in his late thirties broke through the semicircle and proceeded to act like a referee on the fix, siding directly with Gary. "It's one thing to drop you bullshit on some TV show, but what you're doing now is wrong."

Curt could sense the crowd around him, starting to turn against him in their mumblings. "Gary, let me ask you something. This past Christmas when you went to the cemetery, did you not feel the bitter cold all around you?"

"Of course he did jerk off. It was the coldest Christmas on record." The dark curly haired man became more testy and aggressive. He lifted his arm as to push Curt away from Gary.

Curt calmly pulled the man's arm down with his forearm, not showing any sign of intimidation. "EXACTLY," as he turned his attention back to Gary. "It was cold and blustery, you were shivering, you were upset, and you were missing Taylor more than ever. Suddenly, you felt warmth. A warmth that you hadn't felt in a long time. You felt at ease, relaxed and happy. You felt like you were being hugged. Well you were by Taylor. You felt the love and presence of Taylor."

"I was the only one there, how did you know? It was so cold and snowy, that no one was at the cemetery but me. I had my head down and looked up at his stone and out of nowhere, the sun shined on his stone, making his name sparkle with the falling snow. I felt the warmth not just on my back, but all around me. How could you have known?" A humbled Gary reached out to Curt.

"This is what I've been trying to tell people. You weren't alone. Your son was with you. He will always be with you. The only thing your son wants for you is too be happy. He doesn't want you to lose one moment being sad thinking about him. He doesn't want his brother to miss anytime with you. He looks forward to seeing you again. Believe me you love your son now. In Heaven that love with intensify a million times more. Listen, you're gonna miss him, but the day your back together with him, will be the answer to all your questions. Enjoy your life, enjoy your other son, enjoy the knowledge Taylor will always be with you."

"25? Number 25," after a brief pause "26?"

Curt Placed his left hand on Gary's right shoulder. "That's my number," Curt lifted his hand with the ticket "I'm right here." Turning to Gary "Taylor wants you to be happy. We all do." Curt turned and headed to the deli counter "I'll take a pound of the Krakus, please." Curt pointed to the ham in front of him in the display case.

"Bullshit" as the dark haired gentleman wasn't done with his conversation with Curt. "Don't just walk away, trying to make a grandeur exit."

"Umm, I was next." Curt showing his ticket and pointed to the electronic counter.

"What makes you think you have all the answers? There is no Heaven, and you damn well know it."

"What's your name?" Curt asked.

"Why does it matter?"

"I'm just trying to be civil here. Name?"

"Greg"

"Well Greg, nothing more, thank you," Curt received his luncheon meat from the employee, before turning his full attention back to Greg. "I can't change your mind. I have only told people what I know. Maybe being in a coma played mind games on me. But if that were the case, how do you explain how much I know about Gary's son, Taylor?"

"You looked the poor kid's obit up in the paper."

"But Gary approached me."

"I don't know. You tricked him. You're trying to trick everyone. You're trying to trick me." Curt was dumbfounded as he had heard those words before. This time, Curt felt sickened and looked back at Greg's eyes and he knew why. "Leave everyone alone, because you're just causing more heartache."

Greg turned and began to walk away. "I just speak the truth and I know your truth," as Curt reopened the volatile situation.

Greg snapped his body back around, "Oh you do, do you? You don't know shit." Pointing his finger at Curt before he realized the people around him were now staring at him. He turned back around and proceeded to leave.

"Greg?" Greg stopped quickly and stood there with his back to Curt as Curt continued, "I want to say I'm sorry for what happened to you. I'm sorry you had to endure Babe Rafoe." Greg's eyes tightly closed as he felt the blood rush from his face. He hated that name. He always tried to forget, but couldn't. "I know he is the reason you can't play Yahtzee anymore. I know you can't even stomach the sound of dice rolling together. I'm sorry he took your favorite game from you."

The crowd was staring at Greg, as they knew Curt had hit a nerve with this man. They knew Curt was right. "Ba, Babe Rafoe? How could you possibly know him?" Greg suddenly felt sick and pushed a cart to the side so he could make a quick exit from the store. Stumbling out of the store he made it to the parking lot, where he became violently sick.

Curt dropped his basket into a display cooler and followed Greg outside. He placed his hand on Greg's shoulder, but Greg jerked his shoulder's back to get Curt's hand off him. "Greg, you were a kid. You were scared and had every right to be scared. He threatened you and to hurt your parents if you told. You have nothing to be ashamed of. None of it was ever your fault. This man took away your childhood, don't let him take away your adulthood. You're a good man. Please, please live a happy life. We have no control on what always happens on earth. You need to know Rafoe is in the deepest depths of Hell. Heaven will be there for you, but you must overcome this. Don't let it ruin the rest of your life."

Greg looked down at the mess he made in the parking lot. He stared straight ahead for a moment. He then closed his eyes and he felt the rush of love from God pour through him. He stood up, looked up and cried "Why, God, Why?" Greg ran to his car, jumped in and sped off, spinning his tires slightly and unintentionally.

Curt walked to his own car, leaving behind his groceries and a bewildered crowd inside the store.

Chapter 31 Star Light Star Bright

A week had passed since his encounter at Wegman's. Curt still was answering phone calls, but the 15 minutes of fame already seemed to have faded. He had hoped his message was well received, but based on the reaction of the crowd in the studio audience of the VIEW and the crowd in the supermarket, he had to question himself. Curt found himself right where he started 7 weeks before. He was lying in bed.

This time no drool dripped from his mouth. He had energy to get up, but was thinking about everything that had happened over the last couple of months. He did not care if people believed him or even believed in him, but he hoped they did. He just cared that he had done enough to get the message out. "Is there anything else you would like me to do?" Curt stared at the ceiling anticipating a response from God. However, no response was given. Curt did not see any signs around him. Curt did not see a light flicker, hear a bird sing, feel any special warmth on his body, or smell any familiar scents. He could only hear the sound of the furnace kicking on.

He rolled out of bed, made lunches for his kids, had them get up from staying their first night back in their own beds, got them washed and dressed, fed them breakfast, kissed them goodbye as they headed to school on the school bus. He decided it was time to go back to work as he began to work on his resume. He still needed to work, because bills had to be paid and groceries bought. He had been offered to speak spiritually for pay, but he did not want to benefit from what he had witnessed. That did not seem right to him. He worked on his resume until 11:34.

Stretching as he stood up, Curt walked into the family room and turned the T.V. on. The television was on channel 7 and the VIEW was on. "Tonight's the night people." Whoopie was talking to the studio audience. "Tonight is the night; we get our message from God. I'm a little nervous. I mean what do you wear on such a night?" Her comments brought laughter from the studio audience.

"I'm wearing nothing." Joy chimed in. "If we came in the world this way it should be a fun way to go out. Isn't that right people?" Joy turned to the studio audience as they approved.

"Oh, stop it, Joy." Elizabeth responded. "First, we are supposed to get a message, it's not supposed to be the end of the world."

"Who cares anyway? That Schmidt guy never told us where the message will take place. It's all hogwash." Joy was ready to move on to a different subject.

"With my luck, I'll be on the toilet. You know when you get one of those brutiful bowel movements." Whoopie waved her hand back in forth in front of her squinted nose as her glasses teetered on the end of it. "Sorry, God. Let's face it, some people will be sleeping, some will be cooking, some will be making out, and some of us will be on the porcelain squeezing one out."

Elizabeth suggested "That's not beautiful, it's gross!"

"Not beautiful, Elizabeth, but brutiful. You know when you smell your own fart and it smells good, but others find it offensive? It's brutiful. To me…,"Whoopie placed her open had with her fingers touching her chest, "…it's beautiful, to you it's brutal. You know when you're watching a car race and the car crashes, in some ways you are horrified of the brutality of the crash, but in other ways you mind is thinking how cool the crash is. Brutiful. I watch football, hockey and especially ultimate fighting. Man, you can see some brutiful action."

"This conversation is getting brutiful." Joy smiled as she tapped her pencil.

"You're right, let's move on. Remember people, be careful what you do tonight, because you don't know," Whoopie looked up, "who may be watching."

Curt turned the channel to channel 4, "I sure hope there is a message. I know it wasn't a dream I had." Curt sighed as he looked out his family room window at the clear blue sky, "I know it's real. Brutiful, that's funny. Man, this whole experience has been brutiful." Curt smiled, thinking about what Whoopie said. "Brutiful, squeezing one out, nice, real nice!" The phone began to ring with reporters from all over asking Curt if he knew when and how the message would be sent. "We will have to wait and see." This was the only response he could think of giving these calls. Curt was on the phone when his children came home from school. They both hugged and kissed their dad and headed upstairs to play. Curt ordered a pizza in between phone calls and had it delivered to the house. It was approximately 5:30 pm when Curt took his final call of the night.

"Hello, Mr. Schmidt? I'm Darrin McGavin from the New York Post. How are you today?"

"I'm fine. How are you?"

"I'm curious. That is how I am. I want to know if this charade is over and what was the benefit of pulling this stunt?"

Curt was set back by the abrasiveness of this reporter. "This has not been a charade and God won't let me, or what I mean is, won't let all of us down."

"Nothing has happened. The world didn't end. No message was given. No earthquakes, no floods, no hurricanes, no nothing. Should I just report that this was all a scam?"

Curt paused for a moment as there was silence on the line as the reporter waited for a response. Normally, he would have become upset with the rudeness of this man. He would have given it back to him 10 fold worse. This time Curt knew people would believe whatever they wanted to believe. "Sir, I can honestly say, I do not have an agenda. I never said the message would be in the form of a natural or manmade disaster. I spoke the truth. If people do not believe, I can't change their minds. I don't know if the message sent will be seen by everybody or a few. I have no reason to scam anyone, nor do I look forward to any sort of furthering this so called 15 minutes of fame. I know you are cynical and that's okay. People who are cynical will have the most to gain by receiving a message from God. Good day sir and God bless you." Curt hung up the phone and again turned down the ringer. He could understand the man's cynicism.

Curt headed upstairs into the fourth bedroom that he had converted into a play room for the kids. He walked in and his daughter was reading a book, while his son was playing with his matchbox cars. Out of the corner of Curt's eye he noticed something flash outside the window. He walked toward the window noticing another flash outside. Looking up he seen a shooting star. "That's right, tonight is the Leonid meteor shower." Curt spoke out loud drawing his children's attention. "Hey guys, let's get our coats and head up to Chestnut Ridge to see an amazing sight. You can see a whole bunch of shooting stars. Well, they are not really stars, but particles of dust that burn up in the atmosphere, making them look like shooting stars. It's pretty neat. It's called the Leonid meteor shower. At the park it will be a lot darker, so we can see a whole bunch more. C'mon let's go!" Curt picked up his son, lifting him over his head and giving him a razzberry on his stomach, making him giggle.

They went downstairs and put their winter coats, gloves and shoes on, knowing the temperature outside would be dropping into the low 40's. He made some hot chocolate and headed to the park. Outside a few reporters were camped out on his front lawn. "Where are you headed?" A reporter asked.

"I'm taking my kids to..." The thought occurred to Curt that this is where would see the message. "...to Chestnut Ridge for the meteor shower. Come if you like."

"Is this where your message will be sent?"

"I would like to think so. I want my kid's to experience the meteor shower tonight." Curt knew in his heart he would see God's message. He just didn't know at what time.

The Schmidt's got into the car, with the kids jumping in their car seats, as their dad buckled them in. The reporters scrambled back to their trucks. A few of Curt's neighbors, who had come outside, decided to take their families to the park. Soon a stream of car lights headed toward the park. People noticed this line of cars and instinctively turned their cars around and joined the procession.

On top of the toboggan hill a crowd had already gathered. Curt walked his kids to a spot that seemed somehow saved for them. He laid down a blanket and snuggled with his kids as they watched the night sky. People recognized Curt and pointed at him and his kids. Some were ready to leave, but decided to stay, once they seen Curt. Curt pointed up at a few shooting stars flew across the sky and explained in detail to his children about the space dust that entered the atmosphere causing this phenomenon.

"Daddy, look how many there are." Crystal pointed at the number of shooting stars increasing more and more in the night sky.

The particles of dust entering the atmosphere caused a beautiful light show for all to see. The crowd was amazed by the spectacular view they were witnessing. The show lasted for hours. People were so amazed they forgot how cold it was outside. Curt looked down at his phone as he had lost track of time, knowing it was time to get the kids home, because they had school the next day and it was well past their bedtime. Curt didn't realize how far past their bedtime it was when he noticed it was 11:34. "I have to get you guys home," as the phone slipped from his hand and fell facing the time upside down. That's when he noticed that 11:34 upside down spelled Hell. Curt knew this was a message from God. "11:34 upside down is Hell!

So 11:34 upright is the opposite of Hell. THIS IS IT!" Curt stood up holding his son's right hand with his left and his daughter's hand in his right. He realized the Yin and Yang energy he had all his life with his old friend Mike. This had to be it. "PEOPLE, THIS IS IT! GOD'S MESSAGE IS COMING. IT'S COMING NOW!" Curt pointed to the sky while still hanging onto both his kid's hands.

"Daddy, look the shooting stars made a cross." Everyone looked up.

The meteor shower entered the sky downward, then across. Again, more entered downward and across, faster and faster, until the meteor shower was crossing itself, forming hundreds, then thousands of crosses in the sky. The crosses seemed to stay visible for a long time, even though it was just a moment. Then suddenly, the sky was completely black for a moment. While everyone was digesting what they witnessed, a flourish of particles hit the atmosphere again, all at one time. The sky lit up with a simple message. The sky read "BELIEVE."

The crowd gasped as many dropped to their knees and prayed. Curt held his kids tight against him, kissing them both on the tops of their heads. Warmth fell over everyone on this brisk night. God had sent a simple message for all to understand.

People approached Curt, thanking him for allowing them to see the message. A reporter came up to Curt, not to interview him, but to tell him that this message was seen by all across the world. As darkness approached each country a message was sent. The message was read in English, Spanish, French, Arabic, Chinese and the hundreds of other languages of the world. God had kept his promise and the people of the world, kept their faith. The world had changed that night for the good of all.

Chapter 32 Knocking on Heaven's Door

Curt's life was complete after that November night. He watched his kids grow up and start families of their own. He retired from his years of hard, but satisfying work, helping the underprivileged. He had grown old and his time had finally come to pass. "I love you and will love you for always." Curt told his now adult children the same way he always had told them he loved them. He told his grandchildren how he loved them as he kissed each one goodbye. "Celebrate life and I will be waiting to see you in our next journey together." Curt held the hands of his son and daughter, closed his eyes and his spirit disappeared from this earth.

Curt found himself back in all white. "Let the journey begin." Curt began to walk on his long journey back to the Pearly Gates.

"Not so fast," a tall skinny man with a five day growth on his face. "I've changed things around up here, for the better. Heaven is much more efficient now. Just watch." The man moved his hand and in an instant they were both in front of the Pearly Gates of Heaven.

"Are you Steve Jobs?" Curt asked.

"Yes, yes I am. God let me update how we get around up here. Everything is now much more efficient. Heaven is like one big Ipad, for us to move around."

In an instant, Curt was surrounded by his heavenly family that he had missed for many, many years. He hugged his family, reserving the biggest hug for his mother, as he would not let go of his daughter, and waited for the day to see his two other children again, so they could finally be together as one.

The End

www.ingramcontent.com/pod-product-compliance
Lightning Source LLC
Chambersburg PA
CBHW070603130626
46556CB00001B/258